Sweet Possession

NIGHTS SERIES BOOK FIVE

A.M. SALINGER

COPYRIGHT

BOOKS BY A.M. SALINGER

Nights

One Night - 1

The Escort - 2

Tokyo Heat - 3

Sweet Obsession - 4

Sweet Possession - 5

The Proposition - 6

Undisclosed - 7

Hush - 8

One Day - 9

Nights Series Short Story Collection

Twilight Falls

Alex - 1

Carter - 2

Hunter - 3

Wyatt - 4

Drake - 5

Tristan - 6

Miles - 7

CHAPTER ONE

LUKE RUTHERFORD LEANED AGAINST THE SLIDING DOOR that opened onto the sun deck and took a sip of his coffee while he watched the man in the pool. His gaze followed the clean lines of Ash Colby's shoulders and his strong, toned back before lingering on the powerful legs scissoring through the water. Legs that had been wrapped around Luke's hips only hours ago when they were making love and that had gripped his body with savage ferocity when Ash came apart beneath him, his hole quivering and clenching hungrily on Luke's dick while he bowed his spine and cried out in mindless pleasure.

Luke still couldn't believe the gorgeous young man cleaving the water so seamlessly twenty feet from where he stood was finally his. Having doted on Ash since the day he was born and been consumed with desire for him for the last six years, Luke had always imagined his forbidden love for the boy who had grown up looking up to him as a brother was doomed from the start.

Furthermore, as Ash's former guardian and the current trustee of the Colby trust fund, Luke had known acting on his carnal urges would blur the boundaries of acceptable behavior, even after Ash turned eighteen and stopped being his ward. Besides, Luke hadn't ever once imagined Ash would even care for him in that way.

That Ash had been in love with him for even longer than he had, had come as a complete shock to Luke.

It wasn't until Luke had forcibly relocated Ash from Stanford to Singapore two months ago that the complicated charade both men had been playing for the last five years finally came crashing down around them. Uprooting Ash from the only life he had ever known in the US was not a decision Luke had taken lightly, the drastic measure having been forced upon him by the actions of Ash's estranged Aunt Catherine Bernardino—the sister of Ash's dead father, Charles Colby.

Half a decade after Luke squashed the beginnings of a deadly plot that could have ended Ash's life and delivered the substantial inheritance locked in the Colby trust fund to his only living relative, Catherine, the woman had had the gall to contact Luke again to blackmail him. Having paid her and her husband off handsomely to get the hell out of Ash's life for good, Luke had not taken kindly to her threat, nor had he been able to control his rage when he discovered the true extent of the damage the woman who had nearly destroyed his and Ash's relationship had caused all those years ago.

It was only Ash's presence that quelled his burning desire to find and physically hurt Catherine that day. Ash's touch that soothed Luke's agonizing pain at the realization that he had inadvertently hurt the person he loved most in this world. Ash's kiss that transformed the storm inside his heart into a maelstrom of passion that had seen Luke take the young man's virginity, finally making him his in every sinful and sacred sense of the word.

It was also Ash who had abruptly ended the nightmare situation Catherine had been trying to create to extract more money from Luke. Having broken the permanent injunction order forbidding the Bernardinos from making any form of contact with Ash, the couple had had a petition for contempt filed against them in California in the last month and were currently facing jail time. Add to this fresh evidence gathered by the PI firm Luke had had keeping an eye out on them showing the fraudulent investments they had made with the money Luke had given them five years ago, and Luke knew he and Ash had finally seen the last of the Bernardinos.

With Ash settling into his new life at the university in Singapore and their relationship coming along in leaps and bounds, Luke had never known such happiness.

His dick stirred as Ash completed his final lap and climbed out of the pool, sunlight dancing on his glistening, honey-colored skin, and toned limbs. Not only was Luke utterly and blissfully content, he had also never been so completely and utterly sexually satisfied.

Luke had discovered he possessed a high sex drive when he was still in his teens and had bedded plenty of women and men over the years to fulfill his formidable carnal needs. Yet the gratification he found in Ash's arms was something new to him. More than the searing pleasure of being inside Ash's body, more than the fierce orgasms they achieved every time they made love, what Luke treasured above all was the sense of completeness he found in Ash's arms. He had never felt so whole in his entire life. It was as if they were two pieces of a puzzle, made for one another from the day they were born and destined to be together for eternity.

The fiery ardor of their first night together had only gotten stronger in the last two months, with Ash as eager to explore his burgeoning sensuality as Luke was keen to teach him. Seeing Ash discover what a sexual being he was had become Luke's new addiction, as was watching the young man climax. It was a craving that had been too long denied, a secret obsession that consumed Luke whenever they breathed the same air.

Ash dried himself with a towel and headed toward him, oblivious to the filthy thoughts crowding Luke's mind. "Morning." He rose on his tiptoes and dropped a chaste peck on Luke's lips, his steel-blue gaze bright. "I thought I'd take an early morning swim before we started our day. What time is John's housewarming party again?"

Luke placed his coffee on the garden table, looped his arm around Ash's waist, and pulled him in tight before swooping down to take his mouth in a searing kiss. Ash moaned and eagerly parted his lips, letting Luke in. Their tongues clashed deliciously. Ash dropped the towel and gripped Luke's shoulders, his glazed eyes fluttering closed under the sensual assault.

Luke was rock hard by the time he ended the kiss.

"It starts at two," he murmured, his pulse racing erratically.

John Peace, Luke's secretary, had finally given in to his long-suffering partner's wishes and bought a place with him.

"What do you have to do before then?" Ash asked hoarsely, his hips twitching and his erection digging into Luke's left thigh.

Luke swallowed a groan.

You. I want to do you.

Although Luke wanted nothing more than to take the young man in his arms and go straight back to bed to fuck the living daylights out of him, some urgent paperwork needed his attention. Being the head of the billion-dollar Rutherford Industries and the only surviving heir of the Rutherford dynasty meant hardly a day passed when Luke didn't have something to do for work, even on a Sunday. Not that he minded it. He would never have driven Rutherford Industries to the dizzying heights of success they had achieved since he took command of his family business had he not truly been passionate about the job.

Still, Luke always made sure to find time for Ash

since he'd moved the young man in with him. Like having dinner together every night even if it meant Ash coming over to his office in Marina Bay and bringing the meals their housekeeper, Xin, prepared for them when Luke was having a late night at work. Or their lazy Sunday mornings when they would have breakfast out on the sun deck and relax in each other's company.

"I need to look over some documents," Luke said reluctantly. "You?"

Ash grimaced.

"I have a couple more hours to do on an assignment due tomorrow." He wrinkled his beautiful nose. "Remember that international architecture and design competition I told you about—the one in Madrid? Well, my supervisor at Stanford and my new professor here entered me into it without telling me first. The deadline is in six weeks. I have to work on that project as well as all my regular coursework."

Luke's heart swelled with pride. He'd always known Ash was incredibly talented. The fact that the people around Ash were acknowledging this in their own way thrilled Luke like few things could.

He dropped a kiss on Ash's forehead and tipped his chin up.

"You can do it. I believe in you."

Ash smiled, his eyes sparkling with happiness. His expression faltered a moment later. "Shit."

"What?" Luke said, tensing up.

Ash tugged his lower lip between his teeth and dropped his gaze to Luke's mouth. "I really wanna have sex right now."

Luke groaned at the sinfully sensuous look on Ash's face. *This kid will be the death of me.*

"Don't," Luke muttered. "I'm only barely holding on myself."

Ash's eyes widened when his gaze dropped to Luke's glorious erection tenting the front of his pajama bottoms. He grinned and ran his index finger along Luke's hard length.

"What a brave trooper."

Luke shuddered, his cock jerking at Ash's teasing touch. "You're playing with fire, Ash," he warned gruffly.

Ash looked up at him, his eyes darkening, his expression utterly unrepentant. "We gave Xin the day off, right?"

Luke nodded, not trusting himself to speak.

Ash's lips curved in a seductive grin. He raised his hands to his hips and took off his swimming trunks.

Luke's pulse spiked as his hot gaze roamed Ash's delectable, naked body and his straining, flushed dick.

Ash arched an eyebrow. "I bet I can halve the time it takes to complete that assignment. Why don't you look over your documents and come find me? I'll be in the bedroom." Ash licked his lips and palmed Luke's cock lightly. "Waiting for you to sink this—," he tugged playfully on Luke's shaft, causing him to groan, "—so deep inside me, I'll see stars."

Ash headed past Luke and gave him a come-hither look over his shoulder as he sashayed into the mansion, the swimming trunks swinging carelessly from his index finger.

Fuck.

Luke vacillated for all of five seconds before following Ash.

His reason fled when he entered the bedroom and found Ash lying on their bed, fingers already working lube into his ass while he stroked his hard dick, his thighs open wide in an unmistakable invitation, his blue eyes dark and sultry with desire.

Luke was inside Ash in less than ten seconds and brought him to his first orgasm in under five minutes.

They barely made it to John's housewarming party.

CHAPTER TWO

"Ash!"

Ash looked around at the sound of his name.

"Hey, Becca." He smiled at the pretty brunette heading toward him across the airy lobby of the university's School of Architecture.

Rebecca Chan slowed when she reached him. "I loved the presentation you did today," she gushed. "That was an awesome piece of design construction. Would you mind giving me some of the references you spoke about at the end?"

"Sure."

They fell into step as they headed out into the bright afternoon sun bathing the campus, their conversation turning to their most recent assignments and Ash's looming competition in Madrid.

"I really think you can do it, Ash," Rebecca said as they headed toward one of the main drives cutting through the lush grounds of the university. "The other students in our group agree, too. You've been a breath of fresh air to the entire class since you joined this semester."

"Thanks," Ash murmured, his ears warming at the unexpected compliment.

Rebecca paused when they reached a small knoll overlooking the busy road. She took a deep breath and appeared to steel herself for some momentous task.

Ash stopped and looked at her with a puzzled expression.

"So, um," she mumbled, her eyes not quite meeting his, "I was wondering if you wanted to, maybe, grab a coffee sometime?"

Ash blinked as he observed the color flooding Rebecca's cheeks.

"I'm—I'm sorry," he stammered. "I'm already going out with someone."

Rebecca's face fell so dramatically, Ash would have chuckled had her confession not just blindsided him.

"Who is it?" she said, curiosity rapidly overcoming her dismay. She squinted at him suspiciously. "It can't be anyone from campus or I would have heard by now."

Ash nearly groaned.

God, the gossip network in this place is as bad as Stanford's.

"My b—my partner isn't from the university."

Rebecca blinked rapidly. Her mouth formed a perfect "O" a couple of seconds later.

"*Whoa!*" she exclaimed, brown eyes gleaming with delight. She clapped her hands enthusiastically. "So, you're going out with a cougar, are you?"

Ash nearly dropped the folder under his arm as an image of Luke taking him in the shower last Sunday flashed across his inner vision, amber eyes glowing bright with desire as he held Ash up against the black marble wall and thrust powerfully into his body. Ash stifled a wry smile.

Not so much a cougar as a lion gloriously marking his territory.

"Not quite," Ash murmured.

The roar of a powerful engine suddenly cut above the noise of traffic from the nearby road. They turned just as a blue Bentley Continental GT Convertible pulled up to the curb some fifty feet away.

Ash's pulse accelerated as he watched Luke climb out of the car. The Rutherford heir took his sunglasses off and leaned against the vehicle, oblivious to the stares he was drawing as he stood there in his thousand-dollar suit. He arched an eyebrow at Ash.

"Hey, isn't that—" The color drained from Rebecca's face. "*Oh my God!* That's Luke Rutherford, isn't it? The billionaire!" she added with a small shriek. Her wide-eyed gaze swung from Ash to Luke and back again. "*You know this guy?!*"

"Kinda," Ash mumbled.

He was starting to regret accepting Luke's offer to pick him up from campus today. Had Ash realized Luke would turn up in the Bentley looking ridiculously sexy as fuck, he would have declined. Ash was already leery of the covetous looks Luke earned whenever they were in public together. He didn't want a horde of nubile university girls after the Rutherford heir as well.

Ash's cheeks warmed at Luke's heated stare. Of course, there were not many situations when Luke Rutherford didn't shine like the bright diamond that he was. And the fact that he oozed charisma wasn't something he could help either.

Ash sighed.

I bet he'd still look stunning even if he was wearing rags.

Rebecca's eyes slowly widened as she finally registered the charged look they were exchanging.

"Um, Ash. Could it be that *he's* your cou—"

Ash cursed internally at his lack of presence when a knowing expression flared across the young woman's face.

Rebecca clapped a hand over her mouth, her shock turning to uninhibited delight.

Ash swallowed a groan.

"Don't you dare breathe a word about this to anyone. I don't want the whole campus talking about my relationship with Luke."

Rebecca nodded wildly, her bright-eyed gaze telling him that she would keep her promise. She stared in Luke's direction, cheeks flaming.

"Whoa," she said hoarsely. "I bet he's dynamite in bed!"

Ash blinked before bursting out laughing. Rebecca joined him, their laughter echoing to the sky.

"I'm saying nothing," he eventually managed.

"You lucky bastard." Rebecca touched his shoulder lightly. "You'd better go. Otherwise, the look he's giving you is gonna make my panties melt."

Ash was still chuckling when he reached the Bentley.

"Who's that?" Luke said curiously as they climbed inside the vehicle.

"A friend," Ash said. He waved at Rebecca while Luke guided the car into traffic. "She recognized you."

Luke raised an eyebrow. "Did she?"

"Yup." Ash grinned. "There was talk of panties melting."

Luke's lips twitched.

Ash settled back in the leather seat and gazed at his lover. "How was your day?"

Luke smiled. "Good. Yours? How did the presentation go?"

Ash raised an eyebrow. "I aced it, of course."

Luke chuckled.

LUKE LEANED ON HIS ELBOW AND WATCHED ASH's sleeping face in the soft light washing through the terrace doors. They had just finished a two-hour marathon of mind-numbingly great sex, and sweat was still cooling on the young man's body.

He gazed at the graceful lines of Ash's spine and butt where he lay chest-down on the bed beside him and resisted the urge to sink his teeth in the firm twin globes. Although Luke had wanted to fuck Ash for another hour still, he'd promised himself that he'd let him sleep tonight. The young man had another big day ahead of him tomorrow.

Luke's thoughts drifted to the girl he'd seen Ash with that afternoon. The way they'd looked as they laughed together had shocked him and sent a fresh bout of doubt bolting through his mind, joining the host of others that had been there for the past few weeks. Luke couldn't help but think that things were progressing too fast for them. They had gone from being virtual strangers for five years to suddenly living and sleeping together.

Although Luke didn't doubt Ash's sincerity when he said he loved him, he couldn't help but linger on the age gap between them. At Ash's age, Luke had still been sowing his wild oats and had slept with more partners than anyone in his circle of college friends. There was also the fact that Ash had never gone out with anyone before.

Luke had been ignoring the small voice inside him, the one that had been niggling at his subconscious for some time. The one that said this was too good to be true. That Ash couldn't really belong to him. That he was still young. That he could fall in love with someone else.

Seeing Ash with that girl had brought that reality sharply into focus for Luke. Although Ash had admitted he hadn't managed to get hard the first time he tried sleeping with a girl, it could be that he just hadn't met the right one yet. A woman who could fill him with desire. Someone he could marry and settle down with.

Someone who could give him children and a family.

With Colby Corporation—Ash's inheritance from

his deceased parents—now a subsidiary of Rutherford Industries, the Colby trust fund meant Ash would never have to work a single day in his life if he so wished. But Luke knew Ash wanted more for himself than to be one of those useless rich kids who wasted away their parents' hard-earned money. He'd always aspired to bring his design skills to his family's construction business one day and take over the reins his father had abruptly left him all those years ago— hence why he'd insisted on trying out for Stanford.

That Ash would enter the working world with the reputation of being in a same-sex relationship was something that was starting to weigh heavily on Luke's mind. Although being bisexual had never affected his own business dealings, Luke knew his presence and reputation preceded him everywhere he went.

Ash had yet to achieve the same stature in the business world and was bound to be the subject of hot gossip. However open society pretended to be about the gay community, Luke feared it might affect the young man's business ventures when he took over Colby Corp. Even though it physically hurt Luke to admit it, he knew he needed to give Ash some breathing space. It was the responsible thing to do under the circumstances.

Luke stared at the young man beside him and felt his heart twist.

Fuck. I know this is for his own good, but God, it hurts!

He curled an arm around Ash and dropped a loving kiss on his head before settling against him, knowing sleep would be hard to come by that night.

CHAPTER THREE

ASH FROWNED AT THE DRAWINGS ON THE DINING TABLE in front of him. The lines were starting to blur, he was so tired. He rubbed his eyes and looked at the clock on the wall. It was half past eleven.

Luke still wasn't home.

Ash sighed and raked his fingers through his hair.

It had been over a week since he and Luke last had sex. It was the longest they'd ever gone without touching each other intimately—which was a miracle, considering they'd fucked practically every night since that earth-shattering time Luke took his virginity two months ago.

Ash hadn't thought too much of it for the first couple of days. He'd suspected Luke was super busy at work and he hadn't questioned him when he came home after Ash fell asleep and left first thing in the morning before Ash woke up. It was only when Ash realized they hadn't had dinner together for four days and Luke had failed to request that Xin pack a meal for

Ash to bring to his office that he started to suspect the Rutherford heir was deliberately avoiding him.

That was why he'd stayed up tonight to talk to him. It was Friday and, with Xin going away to visit her sister for the weekend, they would have the mansion to themselves.

Ash folded his arms on the table and rested his chin on top of them as he tried to concentrate on his latest assignment.

I should get up and make a pot of coffee.

LUKE OPENED THE FRONT DOOR OF THE MANSION AND blinked when he saw light streaming into the hallway from the direction of the dining room. He locked up and dropped his bag on the console table in the lobby before heading that way. His heart stuttered in his chest when he saw Ash sleeping at the dining table, head resting on his folded arms and back rising and falling steadily with his breaths.

What's he doing up?

Luke studied the dark circles under Ash's eyes with a faint frown. He knew the pressure of the Madrid competition was starting to get to the young man as expectations mounted from every direction. It wasn't just Ash's professors and classmates who were excited at the prospect of the contest, but also the wider faculty at Stanford and the School of Architecture here in Singapore. It would be a major achievement not only for Ash, but also for both universities if he was even short-listed for the coveted prize.

It was one of the reasons Luke had deliberately stayed away for the past week—in addition to his self-made promise to give Ash some breathing space from their relationship.

Like Luke had suspected, it had been sheer agony to keep his own word. Being in the same bed as Ash and not being able to touch him bordered on torture. Luke had barely slept during the last week as he tried to make sure he got home after Ash went to sleep and left the mansion before Ash woke up.

The toll this was taking on his mind and body was starting to show. He'd nearly fallen asleep at his desk a couple of times in the past few days, something that hadn't escaped the attention of his secretary.

"Wow, you look like shit," John said when he'd turned up to work that morning and found Luke already at his desk.

"There are days when the urge to sack you becomes almost too strong to resist," Luke said bitingly. "This is one of those days."

"Ouch," John muttered. "Sounds like someone hasn't had his breakfast. What's wrong? I thought all was good and rosy in the garden of Luke and Ash. Has some snake slipped in and tempted your sweet Eve with forbidden fruit?"

Luke blinked.

"I'm sorry." John sighed, his expression turning contrite. "Michael made me watch a Shakespeare play last night, and I'm afraid the words have stayed with me. I'll probably be quoting sentimental crap for the rest of the day."

"Michael has the patience of a saint," Luke said bluntly.

John sniffed. "That's an undeniable truth. That man wore me down one goddamn flower at a time."

Luke smiled faintly as he recalled the time Michael Woodhouse had started courting John by sending him an anonymous bouquet every day. They'd been worried about a stalker at first. It wasn't until Luke hired a PI firm to look into the matter that they discovered John's private admirer was none other than the head of Rutherford Industries' accounting department, a man who looked like butter wouldn't melt in his mouth and had been blessed with the poker face of a champion gambler. It was hard to imagine that behind that deadpan facade was a fiery, poetic soul who could cook meals worthy of a Michelin-starred chef and tango like a demon. And, judging by the awkward way John sometimes walked into work, fuck like one too.

"So, what's eating you?" John said. "You only ever get this cranky when it's something concerning Ash."

Luke hesitated. "It's nothing. He's busy with the Madrid project right now, so I thought I'd keep out of his way."

John arched an eyebrow. "Really?"

Luke shrugged. "Yeah. So, what's on my schedule today?"

"Lunch with Lana Keele," John said promptly.

Luke groaned. "That woman is like a dog with a bone."

John shrugged. "It's why she became the company president after all. And it's a goddamn good thing she did. Her uncles were driving Keele Industries into the ground. I'm glad her old man came to his senses and passed the reins to her before he died, regardless of the fact that she wasn't the one he wanted at the head of the company."

Luke raked his hair with his fingers. "I wasn't saying she wasn't a good businesswoman. It's just, she really *is* like a dog with a bone."

John raised an eyebrow. "She still hankering after that piece of real estate? The one in the Pacific?"

"Yep." Luke sighed. "Even though I told her it was a gift for someone."

John shrugged. "Well, you can't really blame her. Not everyone's gonna believe somebody would go and buy an entire goddamn island for their lover's twenty-fifth birthday."

His secretary's words echoed through Luke's mind as he watched Ash sleep presently.

Will we still be together then? Three years is a long time.

Luke sighed. There was no point ruminating about things that were still to come. He walked over to the table and shook Ash's shoulder gently.

CHAPTER FOUR

Ash woke up to Luke's light touch and his gravelly voice. He blinked and sat up.

Luke stepped back from the dining table, his expression weary.

"You're home," Ash blurted. He glanced at the clock. It was five to midnight. He narrowed his eyes. "What kind of time do you call this?" he snapped, aware he sounded like a shrewish wife and not giving a damn.

Luke stiffened. His face grew shuttered.

"I've been busy," he said curtly, tugging at the knot in his tie. "What are you still doing up?"

Ash rose and turned to face him, his heart starting a drumming beat at Luke's cool amber eyes. "I was waiting for you."

Luke blinked. "Why?"

A wave of anger suddenly surged through Ash. *This asshole.*

"Let me get straight to the point," Ash said between gritted teeth. "Why have you been avoiding me?"

Luke froze at his stark words. The look that flashed across his face for a split second made Ash's stomach twist.

Luke hesitated, as if he was going to say something. He lowered his gaze, turned on his heels, and headed for the doorway.

"It's late, Ash. Let's go to bed."

Ash stormed across the room and grabbed Luke's shoulder. "Why? So, you can lie there and not touch me?" he hissed, spinning him around.

Luke went still. He straightened to his full height and glanced at Ash's hand where he clutched his suit.

"Let go, Ash," he said quietly.

Ash ignored his warning tone, too far gone to care.

"Why won't you talk to me? Is it something I've done? If it is, just tell me, *goddamn it!*" Ash's voice quivered as he struggled to swallow past the sudden lump in his throat. "I'd rather you be honest with me and tell me the truth, even if it hurts, Luke!"

Luke frowned. "This isn't—look, we've both been busy, me with work and you with the Madrid project. It's not what you—"

Ash swore. "Don't give me that bullshit! We can still make time for each other, like we used to. I can bring you dinner at the—"

"No!" Luke barked.

Ash drew back physically at his forceful denial, too stunned to speak for a moment.

"Have you had your fill of me?" Ash finally whispered between numb lips. Bile rose in his throat when he realized he'd just expressed his subconscious fear. That Luke didn't want him anymore. Didn't love him after all, like he'd claimed he did.

Luke's eyes widened, the expression in them so close to pain Ash wondered if he was imagining it.

"Have you had enough of the *virgin?*" Ash couldn't help biting out.

Luke blanched.

Ash knew the words he was saying were beyond crude and cruel, that he was lashing out from sheer fear, fear that this was over, that he was losing the person he wanted to be with for the rest of his life. In that moment, Ash wanted to hurt Luke just as badly as he was hurting.

"Do you just not want me anymore?" Ash said again, his tone hardening. "Is that it, Luke? Why don't you be a man about it and tell me—"

Luke grabbed Ash's chin in a bruising grip and took his mouth savagely.

Ash's heart thudded painfully against his ribs when Luke bit down on his lower lip before forcing his tongue inside. Ash tasted the sharp tang of his own blood and gripped Luke's shoulders, stunned by the sheer brute strength of the kiss.

Luke wrenched his lips from Ash's mouth seconds later.

"You think I don't want you?" he growled.

Ash gasped when Luke lowered his other hand to Ash's butt and pulled him in. He flushed when he felt Luke's rock-hard cock grind against his belly. Ash's own dick stirred, the feel of Luke's body and his scent so intoxicating after a week of not experiencing either he wanted to whimper.

Luke took Ash's hand and tugged him brusquely out of the dining room. He stormed to the stairs and dragged Ash up to their bedroom, ignoring Ash's mumbled protests to slow down.

Ash's breath hitched in his throat when Luke yanked him across the room and pushed him face to the wall next to their bed. He pinned him there with one strong hand against his nape while he opened the nightstand drawer and took out the bottle of lube and a condom. Alarm darted through Ash when Luke suddenly yanked his pajama bottoms down to his knees. The sound of a zipper being opened hurriedly reached Ash's ears.

"Luke, what—"

Ash stiffened when he felt Luke's hot, hard cock slide against his naked cleft.

"Still think I don't want you, Ash?" Luke hissed in his right ear.

He grabbed Ash's wrists with his left hand and held his arms up against the wall above his head, trapping Ash with his body while he continued grinding against him.

Ash moaned, senses overwhelmed by Luke's forceful hold and the feel of his bare dick so close to his hole. He had never been this rough with him before.

"Luke," Ash breathed, his voice full of need and excitement at the way Luke was dominating him.

He heard the snap of the lube bottle and the rip of the condom foil.

Luke moved back for a moment, his harsh grunt telling Ash he was sheathing himself.

"Oh!"

Ash jumped at the cold feel of lube pouring down his cleft. Luke dropped the bottle on the floor, probed Ash's entrance with two fingers, and shoved them inside the second Ash's hole twitched and started to open.

Ash sucked air between his teeth as Luke briskly worked the lube inside him, his touch gruff while he repeatedly thrust and scissored his fingers in and out of his tight passage, his stiff cock digging into Ash's left buttock, his heated pants washing across Ash's nape. Ash's own dick throbbed and stirred, his arousal sending tingles through his entire body despite the cruel way Luke was touching him.

Luke yanked his fingers out of him and guided his sheathed cock to his hole. He pushed his hips forward and entered Ash in one powerful thrust, sliding all the way in to the hilt.

Ash cried out, the impact sending him up onto his toes. He dropped his forehead against the wall and clenched his teeth as the burn and sting of the vigorous penetration washed through his sensitive passage.

Luke froze behind him, his breath stilling. He let out an animal groan, his fingers going slack where he held Ash's wrists above his head, and started to pull out of Ash's body.

"No!" Ash cried out, instinctively tightening around Luke's shaft.

Luke grunted and swore.

Ash swallowed convulsively, not wanting this to end, whatever it was. The feel of Luke inside him after so long was sending his head spinning.

"Luke, please," Ash whispered.

He arched his hips, his hole gliding back over Luke's cock and taking him inside.

They both groaned at the exquisite sensation.

Luke dropped his face against the back of Ash's head and pressed a gentle kiss to his nape.

"I'm sorry," he whispered, his voice trembling.

Ash blinked, shocked at the emotion clogging Luke's words. He stopped thinking with his next breath as Luke flexed his hips and reached around to palm his aching cock. Ash gasped and moaned as Luke slowly thrust his hard dick in and out of his hungry hole while stroking his shaft, the glide of his clever fingers mimicking the rolling motion of his hips.

Luke continued kissing the back of Ash's neck sweetly as he drove him to two shuddering orgasms. He came just as the ripples of Ash's second climax started to fade, his body stiffening against Ash's back while his cock pulsed and throbbed deep inside his passage, his grunts of pleasure making Ash shiver where his breaths washed across Ash's skin.

They stayed like that for a while, Luke's cock wedged deep inside Ash while he rested against him, his hands supporting Ash's waist, his heart thundering against Ash's back.

Ash whimpered when Luke pulled out of him. He turned on shaky legs and watched as Luke rolled the full condom off his shaft, discarded it in the bin, and zipped up. Luke went into the bathroom, washed his hands, and walked out of the bedroom without meeting Ash's eyes.

Ash's legs finally gave way beneath him. He slid against the wall and landed ass-down on the floorboards, his frozen gaze locked on the empty doorway. He startled when he heard the sound of a car engine.

"What the hell?" Ash wrapped his arms around his bent legs and dropped his forehead onto his knees. Unshed tears blurred his vision. He squeezed his eyes shut and dug his nails into his palms. *What the fucking hell?*"

CHAPTER FIVE

"Wow," John muttered. "Sexual frustration is an ugly thing."

Luke rubbed his temples and glared at his secretary.

"I don't want to hear that from you, Mr. I've Been Fucked Every Night This Week," he said with a grunt.

John startled. "Is it that obvious?"

Luke scowled.

John grinned.

"It's this new vitamin supplement Michael's been taking. It sure—" He stopped at Luke's glare. "Seriously, sexual frustration does *not* suit you. Neither does jealousy for that matter."

Luke sighed and closed his eyes briefly. It had been a week since he'd been home. A week since the night he'd practically raped Ash. A week since he'd been living with the agony of that angry act, unable to quell the storm of regret inside his heart and mind.

John propped his hip against Luke's desk and raised an eyebrow.

"So, what gives? I know you've been staying at a hotel these past few days. Why are you avoiding going home to Ash?"

Luke swallowed a groan. It didn't look like he was going to get John out of his office until he gave him some sort of answer.

"We—" Luke ground his teeth. "We had a fight."

John sighed. "I guessed that. What did you fight about? The fact that you've been ignoring him for the last fortnight?"

Luke blinked owlishly.

"Contrary to popular belief, there is a brain behind this pretty face of mine," John said drily. "So, why don't you tell me what's on your mind?"

Luke inhaled shakily. *It might be good to talk this over with someone.* Still, he hesitated.

John folded his arms across his chest. "I'm not leaving until you tell me what you did, Luke."

Luke's pulse stuttered in his veins. "What makes you think I did something?"

John rolled his eyes. "Because no one is as good as getting in the way of your own happiness as you," he snapped. "Now, talk."

Luke took a deep breath. His words stumbled out, fast and low, as if a dam had broken inside him. He spoke for long minutes. Of his doubts for Ash's future. Of his dread at possibly stopping Ash from having a normal relationship with a woman and a family of his own in the future. Of his suspicion that Ash had mistaken his hero worship for Luke for love. Of his fear that the day would come when

Ash would regret ever being in a relationship with him.

Of the fact that he'd almost raped Ash.

Silence fell across the darkening office when Luke stopped talking.

John rose wordlessly from the desk, crossed the room, and flicked the switch on a floor lamp. Soft light bathed the office as he walked over to the glass wall overlooking the brightly lit bay below. He stood there for a moment before turning to look at Luke, a muscle jumping in his jawline.

"Do you think I'm abnormal?" John said brusquely.

Luke blinked. "Of course not," he blurted.

John pinched the bridge of his nose. "Do you think Michael is abnormal?" he grated out.

"No!"

"Do you think our relationship is aberrant? That our sexuality is sick? Twisted? Immoral?"

"Why the hell are you asking me this?" Luke snapped.

"Because you clearly believe your relationship with Ash isn't normal, Luke!"

Luke's breath locked in his throat.

"I—" He stopped, unable to deny the truth of John's words.

"What is it about me and Michael that makes our relationship okay, but yours sinful, Luke?" John asked quietly.

"He's fourteen years younger than me, John," Luke mumbled.

John shrugged. "So?"

"So, he's still young!" Luke growled. "He was my ward, John. I fucking changed his diapers, for God's sake! He doesn't know what he really wants yet. He—"

"You moron," John breathed, eyes wide behind his glasses.

Luke opened and closed his mouth soundlessly.

"Asshole," John added.

Luke frowned.

"Fucking prick," John muttered.

Luke pinched his lips. "I think you're crossing the line there."

John started pacing the floor, hands waving wildly above his head.

"Man, I pity Ash!" he ranted. "That kid must have the patience of a fucking saint. I would have dumped your stupid ass by now if I were in his shoes!"

Luke gaped, not quite believing John's audacity.

John stopped pacing, stormed across the room, and leaned over the desk. He grabbed Luke's tie and jerked him forward. "Now, listen to me, you dumbass!" he hissed inches from Luke's face. "No one fucking cares about the age gap between you two, except you. Ash couldn't give a flying fuck. As for the rest of the world, well, they can kiss your sweet behinds, as it's none of their damn business. As for Ash not knowing his mind, the kid's been in love with you most of his life. Sure, he worships the ground you walk on, but he loves *you*." John stabbed a finger in Luke's chest. "Not Luke Rutherford, the heir of Rutherford Industries. Not Luke Rutherford, the billionaire. Not Luke Rutherford, the lady and man killer. Just plain Luke. The boy he grew up with and the person he's chosen as his life mate." John scowled. "Ash might be young, but he's fucking smart and ten times more mature than a guy his age should be. So, don't screw this up, Luke. You'll only live to re—"

"Am I interrupting something?"

They both froze before turning to stare at the tall, pretty brunette in the doorway.

Lana Keele blinked her catlike green eyes at them, her expression curious.

"Lana," Luke muttered, strangely relieved to see his former business rival. "I'm sorry. I forgot about—"

"Our date?" Lana arched an eyebrow. "Somehow, I suspected you would. You've been rather distracted lately. Hence, why I'm here." She frowned at Luke's attire and waved the garment bag in her hand. "It's a good thing I brought a tux, too. That suit is sweet, but it won't do for where we're going."

John released Luke's tie and straightened from the desk. "Aren't you supposed to be giving a talk at some swanky business award ceremony in Shanghai tonight?"

Lana rolled her eyes as she crossed the floor toward them, her red velvet dress clinging to her lush curves. "Did Tom tell you that? He's such a little tattletale."

John grunted. "Your secretary is fucking hot. I'm surprised you haven't eaten him yet."

Lana pursed her lips.

"I don't believe in workplace romances. Besides, I'm pretty sure he's gay. Anyway, I asked an old friend to fill in for me in Shanghai. I'm keen to see if the place

Luke and I are going to tonight lives up to its reputation."

John arched an eyebrow. "You just want to check out the men, don't you?"

"Hell yes." Lana sniffed. "I haven't had sex in months. I've even got my lucky panties on."

Luke swallowed a sigh. It was going to be a long night. At least entertaining Lana might take his mind off Ash for a few hours.

The words John had spoken rang in Luke's ears.

Is he right? Am I just making too much of this?

CHAPTER SIX

"That bastard," Ash muttered under his breath.

Xin looked up from the kitchen worktop. "Did you say something, Mr. Colby?"

Ash startled when he realized he'd spoken his thought out loud.

"Sorry, it was nothing," he mumbled where he sat eating at the island.

He'd been doing that a lot this past week. Talking to himself. Ever since that night Luke last had sex with him and disappeared from his life.

Luke had evidently spoken to Xin at some point since the housekeeper hadn't questioned Ash about her employer's sudden absence. Nor had she commented on the fact that Ash was sleeping in his own room again. Even though Xin had changed the sheets, Ash couldn't face being in Luke's bed. His presence and scent were everywhere, a sweet torment and a cruel reminder of how happy they'd been only a fortnight ago.

Ash still couldn't believe Luke hadn't been in touch with him. He knew Luke regretted how rough he'd been that night, but to be honest, Ash had rather liked it. His ears flamed at that thought.

Does that make me a masochist?

Ash always loved the way Luke encouraged him to explore his sexuality when they were in bed together, but he absolutely relished when Luke lost his composure and took him the way he really wanted to. Ash suspected Luke was still holding back on him, afraid he would hurt him if he gave in completely to his urges.

Xin left half an hour later. Ash poured himself a Scotch and sat on the deck to work on the Madrid project. He was pleased with how his design was coming along. The fact that he'd had little else to focus on in the last week to try and get his mind off Luke meant he was going to make the deadline for the competition a week ahead of schedule.

It was gone ten when Ash put down his pen and sighed. He couldn't concentrate anymore. He went to his room, changed into his trunks, and got in the pool. Ash swam relentlessly for half an hour, hoping the physical exertion would wear him out and scatter his restless thoughts. By the time he climbed out, the frustration that had been gnawing at him all week had turned into a slow-burning anger.

That's it. I can't do this anymore.

Ash grabbed a towel and dried himself briskly before snatching his cell from the deck chair. He punched in a number and listened impatiently to the ringing tone. There was a click on the other end.

"Now's not a good time, Ash!" John snapped.

"Where is he?" Ash barked.

There was a pause at the end of the line. "Where's who?"

Ash clenched his teeth. "Don't play dumb with me, John. Where's Luke?"

John hesitated. "I don't think he's ready to see you yet. Give him another day or two—"

Ash swore. "He's lucky I'm giving him another fucking hour!"

"Ash?"

"Yeah?" Ash snarled.

"He told me what happened."

Ash stiffened. The agony of being separated from Luke washed through him all over again, twisting his stomach to knots and bringing bile to his throat. He dropped onto a deck chair, his legs suddenly shaky.

"He did?" Ash said hoarsely.

John sighed. "Yeah. And he blames himself for nearly raping you."

Ash blinked, his heart stuttering in his chest at John's words.

"He didn't rape me!"

"Well, he thinks he almost did and it's killing him."

"But—," Ash swallowed, shocked that Luke had even thought such a thing in the first place, "— it was consensual! And I didn't—I didn't dislike it," he finished on a whisper, heat flooding his cheeks.

"Whoa," John said. "That was too much information." He paused. "You kinky little thing you."

Ash groaned. "Shut up." He raked a hand through his damp hair. "So, where is he?"

Silence descended on the line.

"Promise me you won't cause a scene if I tell you."

Ash tensed. "Why?"

"Just promise me, Ash."

Ash exhaled loudly, not liking where this was going. "All right, I promise. Happy? Now, tell me where the fuck he is."

"There's a new place opening in town tonight. *Le Secret.* You heard of it?"

Ash frowned. "No."

John wavered for a moment.

"It's a high-end escort club. The woman who owns it used to be a professional dominatrix. Luke knows her through Cam Sorvino. Lana Keele wanted to check the place out, so I got them tickets to the opening night."

Ice filled Ash's veins. "He went to an escort club? *With a date?*"

"Well, not exactly a date. Luke and Lana are purely business asso—"

JOHN BLINKED WHEN HE FOUND HIMSELF SUDDENLY listening to the dial tone. "Damn," he muttered, staring at his cell screen. "I should have told him getting into the place is by invite only."

The man beneath him groaned. "I can't believe you just did that. Luke's gonna fire you."

"No, he won't. Besides, he needs a wake-up call, or else Ash really *will* dump his ass." John wriggled his bottom on the rock-hard dick pressing up against him. "Now, where were we?"

He placed his phone on the nightstand, grabbed an ice cube from the champagne bucket, and ran it across the nipple of the man below him.

Michael hissed and flexed his hips.

☙

I'M GONNA PUNCH THAT ASSHOLE WHEN I GET MY HANDS on him.

Ash ground his teeth and glared at the building across the road. *Le Secret* occupied a coveted spot in the downtown area of the city. Ash had only ever visited the neighborhood a few times before, on the rare occasion Luke took him out for dinner.

He studied the doormen guarding the impressive black-and-white metal doors of the venue. A woman stood between them. She wore an earpiece, held a tablet, and beamed a bright smile at the guests pouring out of the limos pulling up at the curb.

Ash glanced down at himself.

At least I look the part.

The gray suit, pink shirt, and purple tie he wore were all ridiculously expensive gifts from Luke. Which was all fine and dandy, but they weren't exactly going to get him into the place. This left him with only one choice. He was going to have to slip inside with one of the other guests.

A limo pulled up behind the queue of others. A middle-aged man with an olive complexion and bushy eyebrows stepped out when the chauffeur opened the back door.

Ash steeled himself, crossed the road, and plastered a seductive smile on his face as he approached the guy.

"Hey there. You looking for some company?"

The man paused and looked over his shoulder. His eyes widened. He turned on his heels and scanned Ash slowly from head to toe, appreciation lighting his face. His gaze shifted briefly to *Le Secret*'s front door.

"You work here?" he said gruffly.

"No." Ash arched an eyebrow. "But I might want to."

The man studied him a moment longer, a predatory gleam in his eyes. He held out his arm.

"Why don't we check it out together then? I think you'll fit right in."

Ash swallowed and allowed him to put his arm around his waist. He masked a shudder when the older man pressed his hand in the small of his back and lightly touched his ass as they waited for the woman with the tablet to check them in.

CHAPTER SEVEN

"Eighteen," Lana said. "In college."

"Sixteen," Eveline Claude said with a smile. "Behind the high school bleachers."

The two women turned and eyed Luke over their drinks, green and blue gazes filled with curiosity.

"Fourteen," he muttered. "In the pantry. With the cook's daughter."

Lana arched an eyebrow.

"She was in college," Luke added with a sigh.

"You dog," Lana said in a disgusted tone.

Eveline grinned.

Luke had liked the feisty owner of *Le Secret* from the moment Cam Sorvino introduced them the last time he was in Tokyo. Eveline Claude was the epitome of a rags-to-riches story, a former escort and dominatrix who now ran her own multimillion-dollar international business catering to some of the richest and most influential people in the world. From what he'd seen of the new club so far, he could tell the reason for her success. With its stunning black-and-white decor, crystal chandeliers, geometrically designed modern furniture, and meticulously attired and attractive staff, the place oozed style and money.

Not to mention it's got downright amazing drinks.

Luke swirled his glass before finishing the last drop of the exquisite cocktail.

Eveline signaled to a waiter from where they sat in a cordoned-off booth and started ordering another round.

"I'm afraid that was my last drink," Luke said apologetically. "I'm driving." He indicated the green-eyed blond working the large, rectangular bar with skillful efficiency. "That guy's good."

Eveline turned and studied the bartender with a warm expression.

"That, he is," she murmured. "Unfortunately, he's on loan for one night only. See that dark-haired guy who's been sitting at the same seat for the last hour? The one who keeps scowling whenever someone tries to chat up Blondie?"

Lana perked up. "You mean, the sexpot who looks like he's got a sizable package?"

Luke groaned.

Eveline chuckled. "Yeah, that guy. That's Joe Cavendish, Blondie's boyfriend. He's possessive to a 'T' and insisted on coming over with Ethan from Japan."

Lana's face fell. "He's gay?"

"Well, bi actually," Eveline replied. "Joe used to be an escort. He owns *Saron*, the most exclusive gay club in Tokyo."

Lana wrinkled her nose. "Any chance he might be available for hire for one night?"

Luke covered his eyes with his hand. "Dear God," he mumbled.

Eveline laughed. "Not unless you want Ethan to stab you in the eye with your Manolo Blahnik. He might look like butter wouldn't melt in his mouth, but he's a real spitfire, especially when it comes to Joe."

Luke couldn't help but chuckle at Lana's morose expression. He turned to Eveline.

"By the way, did Damon & Tucker design this place?"

Eveline blinked. "You can tell?"

Luke smiled. "Kinda. They did my mansion on Sentosa Island."

Eveline dropped her chin on her hand, her blue eyes sparkling. "It seems we have a lot more in common than just Cam Sorvino."

Lana groaned. "Oh God. You guys know Cameron Sorvino?"

Luke and Eveline stared at her.

"Yeah, why?" Eveline said, puzzled.

Luke narrowed his eyes. "What did you do?"

Lana flushed. "What makes you think I did anything?"

"I know you," Luke said tartly.

Lana squirmed on her seat.

"I bumped into him in the lift at his workplace in Tokyo six months ago. I didn't know who he was at the time."

Eveline's eyes widened. "And?"

"I stared at his ass so hard, he looked over his shoulder and politely asked if there was something on his pants," Lana admitted with a grimace.

Eveline nearly fell off her chair as she burst out laughing.

Luke stifled a smile and shook his head. "Un-fucking-believable."

❧

ASH'S HAND TIGHTENED AROUND THE STEM OF HIS cocktail glass.

"Are you okay, sir?"

The blond bartender who'd handed Ash the drink arched an eyebrow at him across the counter.

Ash swallowed and nodded, not trusting himself to speak as he glared across the modern bar to the private booth on the other side of the club. Luke looked drop-dead gorgeous in a black tuxedo where he sat at the table between a beautiful brunette and a stunning blonde, an amused expression on his face as he watched the two women laugh.

Someone touched Ash's back intimately. He startled and glanced at the olive-skinned man beside him. He'd almost forgotten about his unwanted escort.

"Why don't you tell me a little bit about yourself?" the older man murmured, his hand working down toward Ash's ass.

Ash twisted so the man's fingers ended up on his hip.

"Not much to tell really," he said in a brittle voice, his gaze swinging back to Luke and the two women.

"Come now, everyone's got a story," the man said gruffly. "Why do you want to be an escort? Are you broke? Or do you just like sex?"

Ash stiffened when he felt the man's hand slip around toward his groin. He turned and grabbed the guy's wrist, all attempts at politeness dissipating in the face of the anger raging through him at seeing Luke acting like he didn't have a care in the world while he sat there with his two hot dates.

"Look, I'm grateful you let me get in here, but that doesn't mean you can paw me all you want, asshole," Ash hissed.

The man blinked. His expression darkened in the next instant.

"Why, you little shit!" He raised his hand. "I ought to—"

Ash blinked and stepped back.

An arm darted out in front of him. Fingers wrapped around the man's wrist before the latter's palm could make contact with Ash's face.

"Hey there," the blond bartender murmured. Though his lips curved in a civil smile, it didn't quite reach his green eyes. "We do not tolerate violence on our premises, sir."

Fury filled the older man's face. He gripped the bartender's wrist bitingly with his other hand.

"*How dare you!* Do you know who I am?"

The bartender smiled thinly. "Well, I've never seen

you on the Forbes 100 list, so you can't be somebody terribly important."

Ash gaped, shocked at the blond's boldness.

There was a sigh behind him. Ash looked over his shoulder and startled when the brooding guy who'd been sitting on the stool next to him climbed off and towered over them.

"You okay, Ethan?" the stranger said.

The bartender glanced at him. "Nothing I can't handle, Joe."

"You work here, too?" the olive-skinned man snapped at the newcomer.

"No," the guy called Joe replied. He carefully and forcibly uncurled the man's fingers from the bartender's wrist. "But I know the owner and I'm sure she wouldn't want your kind in here." He ignored the man struggling and cursing in his grip, and looked Ash over. "Hey, kid, are you even old enough to be in here?"

Ash opened and closed his mouth soundlessly. "I'm twenty-two!" he blurted out.

The guy narrowed his hazel eyes. "Really? You got ID?"

CHAPTER EIGHT

"Uh-oh." Eveline stiffened in her chair.

Lana followed her gaze.

"Whoa," she murmured. "Your friends seem to be in a bit of trouble."

Luke looked over curiously. The low lighting and music meant most of the guests were oblivious to the scene unfolding at one end of the bar, where Joe Cavendish, the blond bartender's boyfriend, stood holding an angry-looking olive-skinned man in his grip. Joe ignored the spluttering, red-faced figure and spoke quietly to another guy at the counter, a frown on his face.

Luke caught a glimpse of sun-kissed brown hair and a gray suit beyond the blond bartender. He stiffened, awareness blooming inside him. He knew that head and the shape of those shoulders. He'd seen them often enough in his bed in the past two months.

No way. That can't be—

The guy turned just as the bartender moved out of Luke's line of sight.

Luke's stomach dropped when he registered Ash's profile.

What the—

Lana narrowed her eyes and glanced at Luke. "Hey, Luke, isn't that—"

Luke was up and moving before she finished her sentence, his feet carrying him rapidly through the crowded club while his heart started a steady drumming against his ribs.

⁂

"Ash! What are you doing here?"

Ash startled at the sound of Luke's voice. He turned and stared at the Rutherford heir as the latter stormed to his side, mouth dry and pulse a rising beat in his veins, his anger all but forgotten as he breathed in Luke's cologne and his unmistakable scent.

"Now, *you*, I know," Ethan the bartender murmured, staring at Luke.

Luke gazed from Ash to the three men facing them. He scowled. "What the hell is going on?"

The guy called Joe arched an eyebrow at Luke. "You know this kid?" He indicated Ash with his chin.

"I do," Luke said between gritted teeth.

"From what we gathered, he slipped in here with this guy, and the asshole mistakenly assumed that gave him permission to grope him any which way he liked,"

Ethan stated blithely, pointing at the olive-skinned man in Joe's grasp.

Luke blanched. His amber eyes darkened as his gaze locked on Ash's.

Ash shivered at the fury dawning in the golden depths.

Luke took a step toward him. "Are you out of your mind?!" he hissed.

"Is everything okay here?" someone said in a steely voice.

Ash swallowed and dragged his eyes from Luke's livid stare. The blonde and the brunette Luke had been sitting with were standing behind him.

"Joe? Ethan?" the blonde murmured, her blue eyes glittering like diamonds as she glanced between the dark-haired guy holding the olive-skinned man who'd almost hit Ash and the blond bartender.

Joe grimaced. "Sorry, Evie. There was a bit of a situation and—"

"You're that Luke Rutherford, aren't you? Of Rutherford Industries?" the olive-skinned man snapped as he glared at Luke. He indicated Ash with an angry jerk of his head. "Do you know this—this *manwhore?!*"

Joe and the blonde stiffened.

"Jeez, I hope you don't do business with that mouth," Ethan said coldly.

Ash felt blood drain from his face as he watched Luke's expression change. He'd only seen that look of sheer rage on Luke's face a handful of times before.

"Luke," he mumbled.

Luke reached out and took his hand, his heated touch halting Ash's words.

"Yes, I know him," the Rutherford heir told the olive-skinned man in an icy voice, his fingers twining tightly through Ash's. "For your information, his name is Ash Colby. He is the heir of the Colby Corporation and the Colby trust fund—which, last time I checked, was worth fifty times more than what Dimas Construction made last year."

The olive-skinned man paled. His jaw sagged open as he stared from Luke to Ash.

"Now, *that* is a comeback," Ethan said in a voice full of admiration in the stunned silence.

Ash stiffened when Luke turned and locked gazes with him once more.

"We're going home," he bit out.

For one wild moment, Ash thought of refusing him.

Luke narrowed his eyes, as if he'd read Ash's mind. "You either walk out with me or I'm carrying you out of here, Ash," he hissed. "Your choice."

Ash hesitated before dipping his chin tremulously, his heart thundering in his chest. Luke tugged on his hand. Ash stumbled after him as the crowd parted around them.

❧

"Hey," Lana murmured, "are those two—"

"Fucking?" Eveline murmured, her pensive gaze on Luke Rutherford and Ash Colby as they headed for the entrance of the club. "I'd say so." She turned and narrowed her eyes at the hapless olive-skinned guy in Joe's grasp. "Mr. Dimas, was it? I think I can safely say I will be rejecting your application to the club."

She signaled to one of the security guys and watched as he took hold of the spluttering man and escorted him across the floor to a side exit.

"Hey, Joe?" Ethan said, still staring in the direction where Luke and Ash had disappeared.

"Yeah?"

Ethan's gaze shifted to Joe. "I'm kinda turned on right now."

Joe groaned at the expectant look in Ethan's bright green eyes. "What are you? A monkey?"

Eveline smiled as she watched two of the people she cared most for in this world trade light insults.

Lana sighed. "It's hopeless, isn't it?"

Eveline raised an eyebrow. "What is?"

"Every man who catches my eye turns out to be gay," Lana said forlornly. "He's gay." She indicated Ethan. "He's gay." She pointed at Joe. "I bet even *this* guy over there is gay."

"Nope," the handsome bearded man she'd gestured toward stated. He twisted on his barstool and beamed at her, white teeth gleaming against his tan skin. "I'm straight."

"Oh." Lana's face brightened.

Eveline swallowed a groan.

"Hello, Rashid."

"Hey, Eveline," the sheikh replied.

"Excuse us a moment." Eveline tugged on Lana's

arm and led her away from the bar. "Rashid is gay," she hissed in the brunette's ear. "Trust me on this."

"Damn it," Lana moaned. "And I even wore my lucky panties tonight."

"What you need are some toys," Eveline stated firmly.

Lana blinked. "Toys?"

"Sex toys."

Lana blushed. "I—well, I can't deny that I haven't tried a few before, but I don't think they suit me—"

"Look, I feel your pain," Eveline said. "*Everyone* I know is gay, too. And I'm telling ya, girl. You *need* these particular toys."

CHAPTER NINE

ASH TENSED AS THEY APPROACHED THE MANSION. THE drive back to Sentosa Island had taken a ridiculously short time, Luke revving the engine of the Bentley and pushing the speed limit as he raced through the brightly lit streets and across Sentosa Gateway. Although Ash had attempted to engage Luke in conversation several times, he'd only received the odd mutinous glare in exchange, Luke's fury turning his eyes to molten gold.

The security gates opened ahead of them as they approached their home. Luke accelerated up the driveway, the Bentley's beams cutting through the night and washing across the woods that masked the mansion from curious eyes. By the time Luke pulled into the garage, the anger that had been burning inside Ash for most of the evening had started to smolder once more.

Luke climbed out of the convertible and was around the car before the garage door dropped closed behind them. He grabbed Ash by the arm as the latter finished unbuckling, hauled him out of the vehicle, and headed briskly inside the mansion.

"Wait!" Ash said between clenched teeth. "Will you just wait a goddamn minute!"

Luke ignored his protests and dragged him through the house and up the stairs to his bedroom. He flicked on a couple of lamps and stormed across the floor toward the bed.

Ash's stomach lurched, the memory of their last time together sending a chill down his spine.

"*No!* You're not doing what you did last time!" he cried out, digging his heels in.

༄

LUKE ROCKED TO A STANDSTILL. THE RED MIST OF RAGE that had descended across his vision from the moment the bartender in *Le Secret* told him about that asshole groping Ash abated fractionally. It vanished completely when he turned and registered Ash's alarmed expression.

Horror and remorse swamped Luke with his next breath.

Oh God!

He let go of Ash's arm, stunned at what he'd almost been about to do once more. A wave of self-hatred surged through him at the apprehension in Ash's eyes.

Shit. I have to get out of here. I have to get away before I hurt him again!

"I'm sorry," Luke whispered. He raked his hands

through his hair, his wild-eyed gaze locked on Ash's pale face for a frozen moment. He walked past him and headed for the door. "I'm sorry, Ash."

"No!" Ash grabbed Luke's wrist in a biting grip and tugged him around until he faced him once more. He shook his head, his blue eyes bright and burning. "No, I —I didn't mean it that way! I just—I don't want you to make love to me and leave me again!"

Ash closed the distance between them, cradled Luke's face in his hands, and kissed him.

Luke went rigid, shock resonating through him at Ash's words.

"John told me," Ash said against his lips as he gazed up at him. He moved his mouth to Luke's jawline and pressed another soft kiss there. "He said—he said you thought you'd nearly raped me. You didn't, Luke. You could never hurt me."

Luke's gut twisted. He pulled Ash's hands from his face and turned his back on him, unable to look into his beautiful, loving gaze.

"I—but I *did*, Ash," he groaned. "I took you forcefully that night."

Gentle arms wrapped around Luke's waist from behind. Ash let out a shaky breath and rested his head against Luke's back.

"I—I didn't dislike it, Luke," he confessed after a moment. "I loved seeing you lose control like that. And it felt—," Ash hesitated, "—it felt really good," he added in a whisper.

Luke froze when he felt Ash bury his face against his tux. He gripped the hands digging into his belly.

This kid—Jesus, this kid is—

Luke didn't have to look around to know Ash's cheeks and ears would be flaming at his filthily sexy admission. Still, he turned, slowly, carefully, afraid to break this fragile peace between them. He tilted the chin of the blushing young man standing before him and read the amazing, humbling, intoxicating truth in his blazing blue eyes.

"You—" Luke swallowed, unable to look away from the precious treasure that was Ash Colby. "You kill me."

He lifted his hands to Ash's face, lowered his head, and tenderly took his mouth. Luke spent his time exploring the sweet Cupid's bow he hadn't tasted in forever, learning the curves of Ash's lips again, even though he knew them so well he would recognize them if he were blind.

Ash's eyes fluttered closed. He melted against Luke, his breath hitching in his throat, his hands rising to grip Luke's shoulders, clinging to him as if his legs could no longer support his weight.

Luke ended the kiss a long time later, his heart thundering against his ribs. He wrapped Ash in his arms and rested his face against his hair. Peace flooded his heart and mind for the first time in weeks.

John is right. I've been a dumbass.

Fear and regret pierced him then at the thought of how close he'd come to losing Ash through his own stupidity.

Never again, Luke fervently promised himself. *I will never let go of him again. Even if I have to shackle him to me for the rest of our lives.*

"Talk to me, Luke," Ash whispered. He caressed Luke's face with trembling fingers, his eyes full of love. "Tell me what you're thinking. Why you pulled away from me. Why—"

Ash gasped when Luke lowered his head and took his lips in another kiss, this one hot and passionate, tongue sweeping masterfully past Ash's teeth to invade his mouth.

"I will," Luke promised fervently as he sucked on Ash's tongue. "I promise. But, first, I have to wash that man's touch off of you."

Ash blinked, confused.

"What?"

Luke tugged him inside the bathroom and twisted the taps on the rain shower.

"Oh!" Ash startled when Luke pulled him under the cascading hot water.

Luke crowded Ash against the black marble wall and ran his hands down his trembling body.

"Where did he touch you, Ash?" he growled softly.

He dipped his head and nipped at Ash's throat. Ash moaned and dropped his head back, surrendering to Luke's greedy mouth. A gasp left his lips when Luke tugged his tie from his neck and ripped his shirt open, buttons scattering across the wet floor. He flushed, his eyes bright with arousal as he gazed at Luke.

Luke raked Ash's chest gently with his nails before pressing hot kisses to his honey-colored skin, lapping at the water washing down him.

God, he tastes so damn good! I want to eat him up.

"Did he touch you here?" Luke demanded. He

twisted and tugged at Ash's hardening nipples between his fingers.

Ash cried out, spine arching against the wall. "Luke!"

Luke straightened and took his mouth in another blistering kiss, his cock rock-hard where he pressed it against Ash's belly, causing him to gasp and moan all over again.

"Tell me." Luke tugged Ash's lower lip between his teeth and stared into his glazed eyes.

Ash shivered, pupils dilated with passion through the pouring water.

"He—he touched my back!"

Luke undressed rapidly before stripping Ash, their clothes and shoes a wet mess landing softly on the bathroom floor. He turned Ash and pushed him face to the marble wall before hungrily running his hands down his back, reveling in the feel of the beautiful muscles quivering beneath his touch.

"Is this where he touched you?" Luke said huskily, trailing his index finger along Ash's spine from his nape to his cleft.

Ash arched, ass lifting in the air. He moaned when his butt pressed up against Luke's wet, naked cock.

"*Mmm*," he breathed sexily.

Luke kissed and licked Ash's back, taking loving nips and bites of his gorgeous flesh as he worked his way down his body, dropping slowly to his knees. Ash shuddered and arched again when Luke reached the base of his spine.

"What about here?" Luke laved the top of Ash's cleft

and playfully circled it with his tongue while he caressed and massaged the wet twin globes on either side.

Ash hissed and rose up onto his tiptoes. "*Yes!*"

CHAPTER TEN

ASH'S BREATH LOCKED IN HIS THROAT WHEN LUKE parted his butt cheeks and found his hole with his tongue.

"Oh!"

Streaks of electricity jolted through him as Luke flicked and teased his opening with his stiff tongue, probing the twitching folds protecting his passage before gently sucking on them with his lips.

A loud moan ripped from Ash when he felt his body open up to Luke's wicked assault. He cried out as Luke's tongue entered him, toes curling against the wet floor and fingers blindly gripping the marble wall.

"Luke!"

Ash chanted Luke's name over and over again as he continued rimming him, his strong hands holding Ash in place while Ash squirmed and rolled his hips, his throbbing cock leaking pre-cum against the black marble. Ash's belly and balls tightened and clenched spasmodically as the first wave of his orgasm ebbed and flowed closer and closer. He stiffened and climaxed violently a moment later, his cries echoing around the steamy bathroom while he bowed his back.

Luke spun him around while his orgasm still coursed through him and swallowed his twitching, spurting dick all the way to the hilt in one giant gulp. Ash let out a shout at the agonizing pleasure of Luke's hot mouth sucking on his trembling shaft while the sensitive head of his cock slid deep down Luke's throat.

Tension wound through him once more, stiffening his back and legs.

"Oh God!"

Ash wound his fingers tightly in Luke's wet hair where he knelt before him. He rose up onto his tiptoes as he came again, hips flexing and driving his cock in and out of Luke's hungry lips, drenching his throat with his cum while the hot water cascaded down their bodies.

§

LUKE SWALLOWED THE LAST INTOXICATING DROP OF Ash's climax and nibbled gently on his shivering cock as he pulled off and released him, his own dick throbbing so hard it hurt.

Ash sagged against him when he rose to his feet, his head dropping limply against Luke's shoulder, his entire body shuddering with aftershocks of pleasure. Luke palmed Ash's butt and ground his stiff cock against his belly, desperately seeking his own release. He gritted his teeth.

Not enough.

Luke slid his hands down the back of Ash's thighs, lifted him up against him, and wrapped his legs around his hips before propping his back against the wall. Ash gasped and gripped Luke's shoulders, ankles locking instinctively across Luke's butt cheeks.

Luke grunted and flexed his hips, rubbing his cock along the stretch of skin under Ash's balls and nudging his hole. Ash moaned and sank his teeth into the crook of Luke's neck.

Luke cursed, pleasure shooting through him at the delicious sting of Ash's bite and the heady feel of his shaft dancing against Ash's sweet opening.

"I won't—," he ground out, "—I won't enter you. I just—"

Luke groaned and closed his eyes as he took Ash's mouth, hips rolling and sliding his aching cock up and down Ash's entrance, stunned by the wickedly sexy feel of their most intimate parts touching each other nakedly.

Ash wrenched his lips from Luke's mouth.

"Luke?" he whispered.

Luke blinked and looked into Ash's dazzling blue gaze, water pounding down over their heads.

"Do you want me?" Ash breathed. "Like this?" He arched his hips and rubbed himself along Luke's unsheathed shaft.

Luke stilled, his heart lurching at the sinfully bold question. Taking Ash bareback had always been one of his deepest, dirtiest fantasies. One Luke could never admit to Ash before.

He dropped his forehead against Ash's, knowing he had to answer him truthfully. Lying to Ash was never a good plan, as he was coming to realize. It was time for Luke to be completely and utterly honest with the man in his arms, the one he was determined never to let go of for as long as he lived.

"I do," Luke managed between clenched teeth, his pulse racing. "But I won't if you—"

Ash leaned in and kissed him hotly.

"I want it," he whispered, his cheeks flaming. "Take me, Luke. Like you really want to." Ash tugged his lower lip between his teeth and flexed his hips again.

Luke groaned as Ash's twitching entrance stroked the head of his cock.

Fuck!

"Ash, are you—" He stopped and swallowed hard. "Are you sure?"

Ash nodded, his expression turning sultry.

"I want to see you lose control," he breathed.

Ash rolled his hips again and sucked air as he kneaded Luke's cock with his hole, causing Luke to curse. He brought his lips to Luke's left ear.

"I want you to fuck me raw, Luke," Ash whispered, his heated breath and filthy words sending a shiver down Luke's spine.

Shit.

"Hang on," Luke bit out.

He walked out of the shower with Ash clinging on to him for dear life and grabbed a brand-new bottle of lube from inside a cabinet. He rested Ash on the edge of the marble counter spanning half the width of the room, flicked the lid open, and upended it between their bodies, liberally pouring the contents on his bare cock and Ash's spasming opening.

Luke dropped the bottle on the counter and reached down between Ash's thighs. Ash hissed and drove his heels into Luke's lower back as the latter probed his hole with two fingers before entering him. He moaned and rolled his hips when Luke started thrusting in and out, stretching him, readying him for what was to come.

Luke grunted at the wicked feel of Ash's passage clenching around his fingers, dizzy at the thought of what it would feel like wrapped around his bare cock.

"Luke, please," Ash mumbled shakily after a moment. He tightened his hole, causing Luke to curse. "I want it. *Now!*"

Luke pulled his fingers out of Ash and guided the head of his shaft to Ash's opening. He leaned into Ash and pressed his hands against the marble wall behind his head.

Ash wrapped his arms around Luke's shoulders and spread his thighs wide, opening himself up sweetly for Luke's penetration. He cried out when Luke nudged his hips forward and pushed the tip of his cock through his folds.

❧

WHITE LIGHT FILLED ASH'S MIND AS LUKE SLOWLY entered him, the sensation unlike anything he'd ever experienced before, so sinfully hot and sexy Ash knew his orgasm would be upon him within seconds.

Luke's bare cock stretched him beautifully as he slid inside inch by slow inch, taking his time, torturing him with his hot, hard length. Then he was in to the hilt, his balls kissing Ash's butt cheeks. They stayed still for a moment, their ragged breathing loud above the noise of the shower.

Luke lowered his head and gazed into Ash's eyes as he took his lips in a deep kiss and slowly flexed his hips, pulling his dick out almost to the tip before driving it back inside Ash's hole.

Ash gasped, his breath swallowed by Luke, his insides tingling with the first wave of his climax. He came savagely on Luke's fourth thrust, his cries of pleasure muffled by the hungry mouth above him. Luke's golden eyes stayed locked on his as he rode his powerful orgasm, piercing Ash with his molten gaze while he impaled his body with his naked cock.

Luke carried on fucking him slow and deep, the head of his shaft sliding repeatedly against Ash's sweet spot, driving him to a second climax and then a third.

Ash scored Luke's back with his nails as ecstasy numbed his senses, so high on pleasure he feared he'd faint.

"Oh God! So good, Luke!"

CHAPTER ELEVEN

Luke cursed as Ash chanted his name over and over again. He couldn't believe what being inside Ash felt like. Couldn't describe the all-consuming, searing, giddy pleasure of it. The heat, the tightness. The trembling muscles sucking and gripping him, as if they never wanted to let go. The sound of the wet slide of his hot flesh inside Ash's hot flesh. The tingling, aching nerve endings of his cock screaming in pleasure. Luke never wanted this to end. Never wanted to let go of the man shattering repeatedly beneath him, eyes glazed and face flushed with the ecstasy of his orgasms, his incoherent cries and moans a song Luke would never tire of hearing.

Tension spiraled down Luke's back and wound through his belly, heralding his own climax. He slowed his thrusts, fighting it back, wanting to prolong this insane mating.

Ash suddenly spasmed around him, his fourth orgasm so strong his entire body lifted off the counter, his teeth finding Luke's shoulder while he sobbed in pleasure.

Luke swore as Ash's delicious convulsions drove him past the point of no return. His body moved of its own volition, hips accelerating, plunging his throbbing cock in and out of Ash's twitching passage—faster, harder, deeper.

Ash shouted out in ecstasy, his fingers biting into Luke's back, his heels digging hard into Luke's ass, his back bowing.

Fierce waves of pleasure ignited deep inside Luke's belly. He stilled, fingers curling against the wall behind Ash's head, eyes widening at the violent sensations assaulting him. He rose onto the balls of his feet and came violently, ass clenching and hips rolling, his throbbing cock pulsing deep inside Ash.

ASH'S EYES WIDENED WHEN HOT WETNESS SUDDENLY flooded his insides. He moaned with joy as he registered the exquisite feel of Luke's cum filling him, the waves of his own devastating orgasm still throbbing through his body. His gaze found Luke's face. He blinked and stared, unable to look away. At golden eyes flaring wide in pleasure. At color painting strong cheekbones a dusky pink. At powerful throat muscles clenching and tensing. At sculptured lips open on harsh grunts.

The sound of their labored pants filled the space between them as they collapsed against each other,

Luke's arms coming to wrap tightly around Ash, his body shuddering and trembling from his powerful climax.

Ash rested his face in the crook of Luke's shoulder until his racing heart finally started to slow. It was a long time before he managed to raise his head.

"Was that good?" he breathed.

Luke nodded shakily and drew back slightly to look at him. He nudged the tip of his nose against Ash's.

"The best," Luke said, his voice raw with emotion. "That was the best sex I've ever had, Ash."

Ash blushed and bit his lower lip at the ardent light in Luke's eyes.

Luke groaned and took his mouth in a heated kiss. "Don't let go," he murmured.

Ash gasped as Luke lifted him off the counter with his dick still wedged inside him and headed back inside the shower.

Luke pressed his lips to Ash's forehead.

"Let's clean you up."

Ash moaned when Luke pulled out of his hole and lowered his legs to the floor. Heat flooded his face as he felt Luke's cum ooze out of his body and drip down the insides of his thighs.

Luke turned him to face the wall, dropped on his knees behind him, and probed his opening with two fingers.

Ash's breath hitched in his throat as Luke started thrusting in and out of his throbbing passage.

"Um, Luke, are you really just—*Oh!*" Ash rose on his tiptoes as Luke found his sweet spot. "*Luke!*"

ASH SAT ON THE BED WITH A TOWEL AROUND HIS WAIST and stared at Luke. It was past two in the morning and they'd finally left the shower after Luke gave Ash another superb blow job while he supposedly cleaned him up.

"Are you kidding me?" Ash said hoarsely.

Luke grimaced where he sat opposite him. "That's what John said."

Ash shook his head, unsure whether to shout or cry at Luke's confession about why he'd acted like such an ass this past fortnight.

"Un-fucking-believable," Ash murmured as he studied Luke's contrite expression. "You mean to say, I've tortured myself thinking this was all my fault somehow, when you were just being a giant dick?"

Luke sighed.

Ash watched him for a moment before pursing his lips.

"This calls for some kind of punishment," he said abruptly.

Luke arched an eyebrow, curiosity brightening his eyes. Surprise flashed across his face when Ash pressed a hand against his chest and pushed him down on his back. His amber eyes flared as Ash climbed on top of him and straddled his lap.

Ash stared at the sexy, stubborn man beneath him, still reeling from his shocking admission. He'd never doubted they belonged together from that very first night Luke took his virginity. Never doubted that he would want to spend the rest of his life with Luke. To have a family with him, if they both wanted it. To grow old with him.

"You are far too smart for your own good, Luke Rutherford."

Ash leaned down and kissed Luke's chest before biting him, his pulse speeding as he realized where he wanted this to end. It was something he'd been wanting to try for a while.

Luke flexed his hips, his cock stirring under the towel covering his groin and nudging the inside of Ash's left thigh.

"Let me make one thing clear," Ash murmured, his mouth finding Luke's left nipple. He kissed and licked it before tugging on it with his teeth.

Luke grunted and grabbed Ash's waist, fingers biting into his skin.

Ash made his way to Luke's right nipple and administered the same sweetly cruel treatment before working his way down Luke's six-pack.

"Just because I'm younger than you doesn't mean I don't know my own mind."

Luke cursed when Ash dipped his tongue inside his navel, the hard muscles of his belly quivering under Ash's dancing fingers.

"I know who I am and what I want."

Ash looked down at the shape of Luke's arousal denting the fabric of the towel below him, anticipation sending blood roaring in his ears. He tugged the material from Luke's hips and dropped the ends on the bed, uncovering him.

"And that's you, Luke."

Ash leaned down and kissed Luke's shaft before taking his dick in his hands.

"Ash!" Luke growled. He lifted his head off the bed and looked down his body to where Ash cradled his cock in his fingers, his expression half-shock, half-sinful expectation.

Ash kept his eyes on Luke's amber gaze as he opened his mouth and licked the glistening head of Luke's dick.

"*Fuck!*" Luke gasped. He grasped the sheets in a white-knuckled grip, his entire body going rigid.

"What I want is you," Ash repeated. His heart pounded at the exquisite feel and taste of Luke. "All of you."

CHAPTER TWELVE

Oh God!

Luke's eyes almost rolled back in his head as Ash took him inside his mouth. He could hardly believe Ash was fulfilling every single one of his dirty fantasies in this one night. At this rate, he was going to have a coronary by the time dawn came.

Ash moaned and started working Luke's dick with his fingers, lips, and tongue, mimicking what Luke had done to him countless times before.

Yup, Luke thought dazedly as pleasure stabbed through him with each contraction of Ash's strong jaw and eager flick of his tongue, *the kid is a brilliant student all right.*

Ash grunted as he tried to swallow Luke to the hilt.

Luke looked down his body and nearly cursed at the filthy vision of Ash's head bobbing up and down his cock. He caressed Ash's chin gently with one hand, his belly clenching in anticipation.

"Breathe through your nose and try to relax your throat."

Ash glanced up at him and nodded, the motion sending Luke's dick deeper in his mouth.

Luke swallowed as he watched Ash try to take him all the way inside. He felt his dick touch the back of Ash's throat and bit back a grunt when Ash gagged.

"It's okay. You don't have to—"

Ash let go of Luke's dick with a popping sound that made him curse.

"But I want to," he said, hands finding Luke's shaft once more.

Luke would have laughed out loud at Ash's petulant expression had he not looked so obscenely sexy where he straddled Luke's thighs and worshipped his dick with his clever fingers.

Ash frowned at Luke's cock. "Maybe if I try another position?"

Luke covered his face with his hands and groaned.

It's official. This kid is gonna kill me.

"You really want to do this so badly?" he said between clenched teeth.

"Well, yeah," Ash muttered. "I mean, it feels unreal when you do it to me and you look like you really enjoy it, so…"

Luke rose onto his elbows and gazed at Ash's flushed expression, his heart drumming against his ribs.

"Kneel on the edge of the bed," he said hoarsely.

Ash blinked. He shuffled to the edge of the mattress

while Luke climbed off and came to stand opposite him.

Luke looked down into Ash's heated gaze and cupped his chin with his hand. "Lift your head higher."

Ash obeyed, arching his neck until he was looking straight up at him, his face perfectly aligned with Luke's groin.

Luke guided the tip of his cock to Ash's mouth and gently stroked the head against his lips. Ash's eyes darkened with excitement. His tongue flicked out and laved Luke's flushed, sensitive skin.

Luke hissed in pleasure. He curled his fingers in the back of Ash's head and nudged his hips forward.

Ash kept his eyes locked on Luke's as he opened his mouth and took him in.

Luke shuddered, pleasure shooting through him.

"Open your jaw wider." He groaned as Ash obeyed. "Yes, like that."

Ash moaned as Luke's dick went in even deeper. His eyelids fluttered closed.

Luke's heart slammed against his ribs as he stared at the sexy vision of the man beneath him.

"Now, breathe slowly through your nose and try relaxing your throat again."

Ash grunted and did as he'd been instructed.

Luke tugged his lower lip between his teeth at the agonizing sensation of Ash slowly swallowing him to the hilt. He stayed still for a moment, letting Ash adjust to the new feeling. Then, he gripped Ash's head lightly and gently withdrew his cock from his mouth before sliding back inside.

Ash inhaled through his nose and gulped him in.

Holy—

Luke couldn't take his eyes off Ash as he slowly fucked his throat. The sight of his glistening wet dick sliding in and out of Ash's lips and bulging his cheeks was so arousing, it was a miracle he didn't come there and then.

Heat soon coiled along Luke's thighs and pooled in his lower back. Tension tightened his belly with each glide and thrust of his cock inside Ash's mouth and throat, the waves spiraling closer and closer until they became a surging, gathering tide.

Luke felt his balls contract and knew he was close to his climax.

"Ash, let go."

He cradled Ash's chin with one hand and started to pull out.

Ash frowned and grabbed Luke's hips, fingers biting into his flesh. He grunted and clamped down on Luke's dick with his lips while he continued moving his head to and fro, maintaining his sinful, exquisite assault.

"Ash," Luke said huskily. His toes curled against the floorboards as the first wave of his orgasm danced down his spine.

Ash opened his blazing, cobalt blue eyes and stared up at Luke as he deep-throated his dick to the hilt.

It was all too much for Luke.

He twisted his fingers in Ash's hair and gave in to his body's instinct, bowing his back and jerking his hips as he came, harsh grunts leaving his lips, his buttocks clenching painfully while the savage orgasm drove him up onto the balls of his feet.

Ash's moans echoed his guttural noises as he swallowed and sucked eagerly on Luke's pulsing dick.

Luke relaxed back on his feet a while later, body still trembling from the intensity of his climax. He pulled his aching, sensitive flesh from Ash's mouth and pushed him back onto the bed before climbing on the mattress. Ash parted his thighs and welcomed Luke into the cradle of his body as they settled down on a pillow.

Luke kissed the flushed young man beneath him passionately, his salty cum on Ash's tongue sending a thrill through him.

"Did that—," Ash started shyly when Luke ended the kiss, "—did that feel good too?"

Luke groaned at Ash's hesitant expression.

"*Everything* you do to me feels good, Ash. In fact, it's beyond good." He moved his mouth to Ash's left ear, licked the shell, and gently bit the lobe. "You fulfill me, body and soul. And I'm never letting you go."

Ash shivered beneath his touch and gripped his shoulders hard.

"Promise?" he said tremulously.

Regret stabbed through Luke as he pulled back and read the lingering doubt in Ash's eyes. He bowed his back and pressed a kiss over Ash's heart, reveling in the feel of the strong beat beneath his lips, vowing to spend the rest of his life cherishing the precious man in his arms so he would never again feel uneasy about exactly how much Luke cared for him.

"I promise," Luke vowed in a heartfelt voice.

CHAPTER THIRTEEN

"Oh my." Xin rocked to a standstill in the middle of the lounge, a tray of appetizers in hand.

Lana Keele sneaked up on her and stole a prawn from one of the dishes. "They're quite a sight, aren't they?"

Xin stared at the men sitting around the pool and on the patio of the mansion's rear garden before dipping her chin slightly.

Luke walked around the bar and handed Lana a drink.

"Are you all right, Xin?" he said, puzzled.

Xin nodded wordlessly before heading out onto the deck, her ears red.

"I believe your housekeeper is somewhat overwhelmed by how jaw-droppingly gorgeous your guests are," Eveline Claude said wryly as she reached for the cocktails on the counter.

Luke looked through the open patio doors.

Ash was at the garden table with Gabe Anderson,

Cam Sorvino's fiancé, and Ethan Skye, the blond bartender who'd saved Ash from the unwanted attention of his admirer at the grand opening of *Le Secret*.

Ethan's boyfriend, Joe, and Cam, Joe's best friend, lounged by the pool, legs dangling in the water as they chatted.

It was a sunny Saturday afternoon in early December, a month following the night Luke and Ash finally made up. Luke had invited the men and women over on a rare weekend when all of them happened to be in town.

A warm feeling filled Luke's chest as he gazed lovingly at Ash where he sat talking animatedly to Gabe and Ethan. The happiness of their everyday life since they'd fully committed to one another on that fateful night had Luke walking on cloud nine most days. He could hardly believe such bliss existed. Now that he had finally put his fears to rest and completely opened his heart to Ash, their relationship had deepened and grown even more intimate, both in and out of the bedroom.

Luke smiled faintly. "He's pretty special."

Lana gaped at him. "Good God, I never thought I'd see the day Luke Rutherford would act like a besotted fool."

Luke arched an eyebrow at her. "Jealousy is an ugly thing, Lana."

Lana made a face. Eveline chuckled. They followed him out onto the deck.

Ash looked up at Luke warmly as he and Eveline

brought their drinks to the table. "Did you know Ethan was at Stanford too?"

Luke studied the blond bartender appraisingly. "I didn't."

Gabe and Eveline shared a grin.

"Ever heard of an elusive investment genius by the name of Mr. S?" Eveline said innocently.

Ethan groaned. "Seriously, you guys need to learn to shut up. I am never entrusting you with a secret again."

"What secret?" Joe said as he came over. He took a sip from Ethan's glass and settled on the armrest of his chair, his hand resting casually on the younger man's right shoulder.

"Something about a Mr. S?" Ash said, puzzled.

"Yeah, I've heard of him," Luke said, equally intrigued.

Cam groaned as he approached the table. "Not that damn Mr. S again."

Gabe handed him a drink.

"Thanks." Cam dropped a kiss on Gabe's head.

Gabe smiled.

"Have I ever told you that your husband-to-be is an ass?" Ethan asked Gabe pointedly.

Gabe laughed. "Like, every time we see each other."

"So, who's this Mr. S?" Ash said. "And what does it have to do with Ethan being at Stanford?"

"Mr. S is in the top one percent of the most lucrative investors in the world right now and is one of my firm's clients," Cam said with a grunt. "When it comes to stocks and shares, very few people can beat him." He narrowed his eyes at Ethan. "He's also a smart-mouthed so-and-so who graduated summa cum laude from Stanford business school and moonlights as a bartender."

Luke stared at Ethan, surprised. "*You're* Mr. S?"

"Wow, looks *and* brains," Lana muttered.

Ethan's ears grew red.

"Christ, we might as well put out a public service announcement at this rate," he muttered.

Joe chuckled, hazel eyes dancing with delight at his lover's embarrassed expression.

The sound of a bell came faintly in the distance. Luke turned toward the mansion and caught a glimpse of Xin heading for the intercom linked to the front gates.

"I wonder who that is," he murmured.

He headed into the property while Ash and their guests continued chatting on the patio. A delivery van was pulling up to the drive when he reached the main entrance.

"It's okay, Xin," Luke said. "I'll handle this."

Xin nodded and disappeared in the direction of the kitchen.

The van braked to a stop. A young woman jumped out of the driver's seat and came around the front of the vehicle. Her gaze moved from the mansion to Luke. She blinked.

"I have a, er, delivery for Mr. Colby," she murmured, cheeks flushing.

"I'll take it." Luke watched curiously as she opened the side door of the van, removed a large package, and handed it to him. It was surprisingly light and came with a letter.

Luke's pulse stuttered when he registered the return address. He signed the delivery card, thanked the woman, and headed back inside the mansion with the parcel, his heart drumming against his ribs.

"Ash, you've got a delivery," he said in a level tone as he walked out onto the patio.

Ash's eyes widened when he looked over. "What the—"

He rose to his feet while Luke carefully placed the package on a deck chair. Luke wordlessly handed him the envelope.

Ash paled when he read the back of it.

"Luke," he breathed, steel-blue eyes glittering with a mixture of apprehension and excitement.

Their friends watched them, puzzled.

"What is it?" Eveline said, glancing between the two of them.

Luke masked his own nervousness behind a smile. "Open it."

Ash's hands trembled as he peeled the flap back. He took out the letter inside and unfolded it. His eyes widened as he read it.

"Ash?" Luke said, his mouth dry.

Ash stared at him, dumbfounded. "I—I won," he breathed.

"Won what?" Gabe said.

Ash handed Gabe the letter just as Luke closed the distance between them and cradled his face in his hands.

"Congratulations," Luke whispered, his heart full to bursting with happiness and pride. He lowered his head and took Ash's mouth in a sweet kiss, unheeding of their guests. "I'm so thrilled for you, Ash."

Ash's eyes glittered as he looked up at Luke, his face full of emotion.

"Holy shit." Gabe straightened in his seat and stared from the letter to Ash, his face full of admiration.

"What?" Ethan said, his curious expression reflected on the others' faces.

"There's an annual architecture and design competition based out of Madrid," Gabe explained. "It's open to the hottest new graduates the world over and is among the most highly regarded awards in the business. Even making the shortlist is a privilege and pretty much guarantees the candidate will be headhunted by the best architectural design firms in the world." He grinned at Ash. "You're looking at this year's competition winner."

Ash flushed when everyone on the deck clapped and cheered for him. Luke cleared a space on the table and brought the package over from the deck chair. Ash's hands shook as he carefully opened it under their watchful gazes.

CHAPTER FOURTEEN

LUKE'S BREATH CAUGHT IN HIS THROAT. HE STARED AT the exquisite model the competition organizers had made from Ash's design, stunned beyond words. The building was a sleek, modern geometric pavilion set within a beautifully sculptured landscape. Made of glass, wood, concrete, and metal, it demonstrated an artful mix of the old and the new, with a unique contemporary look that still exhibited warmth and charm.

"Wow," Ethan said, eyebrows rising so high they almost touched his hairline.

"It's gorgeous, Ash." Gabe dropped down onto his haunches to examine the model. He ran his fingers lightly along the streamlined angles, his blue eyes sparkling. "You truly deserve this win."

"Thanks," Ash murmured shyly as everyone congratulated him once more.

Had it not been for the presence of their guests,

Luke would have swept Ash up into his arms and taken him upstairs to their bedroom.

It wasn't until later that evening, after the party had ended and their friends and Xin had left, that Luke finally had Ash all to himself. They sat out by the pool for a while, Ash lying on Luke where he lounged on a deck chair, their gazes on the star-filled sky above them as they chatted lightly and finished the last of the champagne Luke had opened to celebrate Ash's winning the competition.

"Luke," Ash muttered after some time.

"Yeah?"

"That's a pretty impressive hard-on I can feel against my ass."

Luke chuckled and tightened his arms around Ash. "I'm surprised it took you so long to notice."

"Oh, I noticed all right," Ash countered drily. He twisted in Luke's arms. "Want to go to bed?" he said, his voice turning husky as he looked down at him.

Luke rose onto his elbows and kissed the tip of Ash's nose. "I thought you'd never ask."

Ash climbed off him and held his hand out. Luke twined his fingers through Ash's and rose to his feet. They headed into the mansion, their pace unhurried as they made for the stairs and climbed the steps to their bedroom. Luke flicked the lamp on the nightstand and turned to see Ash peeling his T-shirt up over his head. He closed the distance between them and took Ash's mouth in a long, deep kiss, fingers running lightly up and down Ash's bare chest and arms. Ash shivered and arched into his touch, his tongue dancing sweetly with Luke's, a small moan of need escaping his throat.

They undressed slowly, not wanting to break their kiss, their mouths seeking each other every time their lips parted even for an instant.

Luke took Ash's hand and led him onto their bed. He moved him gently down onto his back and settled his powerful frame on top of him. Ash parted his thighs and welcomed Luke into the cradle of his body, his arms rising to coil around Luke's shoulders. Luke leaned his elbows on either side of Ash and kissed him over and over again.

By the time he moved his lips to Ash's ear, the latter was clinging passionately to him, his erection rubbing against Luke's belly, his heated pants resonating around the room.

"Luke," Ash breathed, voice full of hunger and fingers biting into Luke's back.

Luke lovingly kissed and bit Ash's earlobe before shifting to the beautiful arch of his throat, the young man's taste so intoxicating he wanted to drown in it. He lingered on Ash's strong pulse and delighted in the way it jumped and skittered beneath his touch.

Ash twined his hands in Luke's hair as he worked his way down his body, knees rising and dropping open in an unconscious invitation. Luke licked and teased Ash's belly until the latter groaned out loud, his fingers trailing tantalizingly up and down Ash's trembling thighs, his own heart racing in anticipation of their lovemaking.

"Luke!"

"Yes, Ash?" Luke murmured, knowing full well what he wanted but needing to hear it still.

"Touch me," Ash moaned, urging Luke's head south with his hands. "Down there."

Luke didn't have to be asked twice. He bowed his back and kissed the tip of Ash's straining dick.

Ash cried out and flexed his hips off the bed.

Luke shifted on the mattress, nudged his shoulders under Ash's thighs, and gripped the backs of his knees. He pushed Ash's legs up toward his chest and flicked the sensitive head of his cock with his tongue before circling and ardently laving it.

Ash let go of Luke's head and fisted his hands in the sheets on either side of the pillow. His breath hitched in his throat when Luke ran his tongue from the base of his cock all the way to the tip and back again.

"*Oh!*"

Luke grunted and took Ash's twitching shaft in his mouth, swallowing him to the hilt in one smooth glide. He used his lips and tongue and throat to pleasure him, reveling in Ash's mindless cries and moans and the way his entire body tensed and shuddered repeatedly below him.

It wasn't long before Ash climaxed, his hot cum hitting Luke's taste buds while his heady scent flooded his senses. Luke milked him to the very end and didn't let go for a long moment, tongue teasing his trembling balls and teeth nibbling his throbbing shaft.

Ash collapsed down on the bed when Luke finally released him, his body coated in a fine sheen of sweat.

Luke licked the salty drops on his belly and chest as he made his way back up his body, his own dick doing press-ups against the mattress between Ash's legs. He reached for the nightstand drawer and grabbed blindly for the bottle of lube as Ash reached up and tugged his head down for a hot kiss.

"Luke," Ash whispered sweetly against his lips, his steel-blue eyes dark with desire.

He wrapped his thighs around Luke's waist and arched his hips into him as the latter opened the bottle and poured the cool liquid in one hand.

Luke bit back a groan, propped his left elbow by Ash's right ear, and liberally coated his bare cock with the lube before reaching down between their bodies.

Ash panted loudly when Luke pressed his slick fingers to his hole and teased his folds. *"Mmm."*

Luke's dick throbbed at the breathy little sounds Ash made when he slowly penetrated him. He leaned down to swallow Ash's rising moans with his lips as he started thrusting his fingers in and out, his own grunts of pleasure at the way Ash's hot passage sucked and squeezed him muffled between their lungs.

Ash wrenched his lips from Luke's mouth a moment later.

"Luke, please," he begged, his cheeks flushed and his eyes bright with arousal. "Enter me!"

Luke's heart twisted at the erotic image of Ash beneath him. He gripped Ash's legs and pushed them up, dropping his calves onto his shoulders. Ash gasped at the way this opened him further, his expression thrilled. His lips parted on a guttural groan as Luke brought the tip of his naked cock to his opening and slowly pushed in.

"Oh!"

Ash closed his eyes and arched his spine, an expression of intense pleasure flooding his face.

Luke bit his lip at the staggeringly exquisite feeling of being inside Ash. However many times he'd taken Ash bareback since that first night, each time still felt like the first all over again. He rose up onto his hands and dropped a hot kiss on the inside of Ash's right thigh as he started their intimate dance, knees supporting his weight while his hips rolled and thrust his cock slow and deep into Ash's hot, trembling passage, repeatedly nudging his sweet spot.

Ash raked Luke's back with his nails, his cries growing more incoherent, his heels digging into Luke's shoulder blades. He climaxed a moment later, his hole spasming deliciously around Luke's throbbing dick, sucking him in tight.

Luke grunted and maintained his sensuous assault, bringing Ash to a second and third orgasm. His own climax swirled tantalizingly at the base of his spine, slow waves that ebbed and flowed, gathering in strength with each contraction of Ash's quivering passage until he reached the point of no return. Luke came savagely, back bowing and body stiffening above Ash, his grunts joining Ash's cries as blinding pleasure pulsed through him.

Sweat dripped off Luke's chin and landed on Ash's

chest as his cock jerked and pulsed cum deep inside him. He brought Ash's legs down to his waist, curled his arms under his back, and lifted him up as he sat back on his heels.

CHAPTER FIFTEEN

ASH GASPED AS HE FOUND HIMSELF UPRIGHT AND straddling Luke's lap, dizzy from the fierce orgasm still shuddering through him. Luke lifted his head and kissed Ash hotly as he continued thrusting his rock-hard shaft into Ash's body, his eyes bright and golden.

"Oh! Mmm!"

Ash moaned and dropped his heels to the mattress. He rode Luke's cock, rising up as Luke pulled out and dropping down as Luke rammed his hips up, their tempo matching flawlessly. He bit his lower lip at the intense penetration, searing flashes of pleasure tearing across his inner vision. Fierce tension coiled through him once more, his belly clenching so tightly it was almost painful.

Luke accelerated his pace, his fingers biting into Ash's flesh, his pants heralding his own climax.

Ash stiffened and dropped his head back as he came violently, his insides clenching and convulsing while he ejaculated hot cum between their bodies, his cries of ecstasy echoing across the room.

Luke's teeth found his throat. He let out a guttural groan and held Ash's hips in place while he climaxed, his cock pumping his release deep inside.

Ash gasped and shuddered at the hot wetness flooding his passage. He relished this—this filthy, sexy feeling of Luke taking him bareback and filling him with his seed. It made him feel branded and whole at the same time, finally secure in the knowledge that Luke would never leave his side.

They rested against each other in the aftermath of their powerful lovemaking, hands tightly cradling one another, bodies trembling with aftershocks of pleasure.

"I love you, Ash," Luke whispered. He lifted his head from Ash's chest and looked up at him, his amber eyes full of emotion. "So goddamn much."

Ash swallowed, his vision blurring. "I love you too, Luke."

Luke kissed him sweetly. Ash moaned as Luke rose onto his knees and climbed off the bed with his arms around him, his cock still buried inside Ash's passage. He headed into the bathroom and gently cleaned Ash before washing the sweat off their bodies. They dried each other off and collapsed back on the bed, Luke wrapping his arms around Ash as the latter rested his head on his chest.

Ash sighed. "Is it possible to go crazy from happiness?"

Luke chuckled. "I hope not. Otherwise, they'll have to lock both of us up."

Ash hesitated before raising his head and looking at Luke. "You know the pavilion I made for the competition? I—" He stopped, ears flushing as he wondered if his confession would sound too sappy.

Luke kissed the tip of his nose, his expression curious and encouraging at the same time. "What is it?"

"I designed a smaller version of it. A home." Ash blushed. "I thought we could live in it one day." He blinked rapidly. "Not here. I love this mansion!" he added hastily. "But, if we ever go back to California, I—"

Ash gasped when Luke cupped his face and kissed him hotly.

"You really will drive me insane with happiness," Luke groaned against his lips.

Ash smiled tremulously, his chest so tight with bliss he thought his heart would burst.

Luke suddenly looked sheepish. "How about the Pacific?"

Ash stared. "What?"

❧

LUKE GRINNED. "I KNOW SOMEWHERE WE COULD BUILD this place." He rolled to the edge of the mattress and grabbed his cell from his shorts pocket.

Ash knelt on the bed while Luke sat up and tapped the screen. He brought up a satellite map and showed it to him.

"You weren't supposed to find out about this place until your twenty-fifth birthday. The day you inherit your trust fund," Luke admitted quietly. "But I think this would be perfect for the pavilion."

Ash stared at the dot on the sea of blue, still puzzled. "What am I looking at?"

"An island," Luke said. "Your island, Ash."

Ash's breath hitched in his throat. "*What?!*"

Luke smiled. "John said I was crazy, but hell, I don't care." He dropped a kiss on Ash's forehead. "Happy early twenty-fifth birthday, Ash."

Ash blinked, stunned beyond words.

"The guys who designed this mansion would be thrilled to get this project," Luke added huskily. "Gabe works for them, too."

"I—I don't know what to say," Ash whispered.

He stared from Luke to the cell screen, his expression turning thoughtful.

"This could be the flagship concept for relaunching the Colby Corporation." Ash looked steadily at Luke. "I want to take my father's company in a new direction. Make it my own." He bit his lower lip. "Make it ours."

Luke kissed him again. "I'm all for it. Whatever you want and need, Ash, I'll be here for you."

Ash nodded and swallowed. "I'll start slow. I don't want to waste the trust fund money." He stopped and stared when Luke grinned at him. "What?"

"You have more than enough money to do what you want, Ash." Luke dropped another kiss on his nose. "In fact, last time I checked, Colby Corp and your trust fund were worth over five billion dollars."

Ash paled. "What? But—but, *how?!* It was only

valued at two hundred and fifty million when my parents died!"

"I invested it for you," Luke explained. "And it's grown even more since Cam took over. He's working solely on your trust fund, Ash."

Ash blinked.

Luke hesitated then. He tilted his head toward the satellite map on his phone. "The island. I think—" He paused and inhaled deeply, suddenly nervous. "I think it would be a great place to have our wedding one day."

This time, Ash couldn't hold back his cry of joy. He dropped the cell on the bed, wrapped his arms around Luke's shoulders, and kissed him hard.

"I don't know what I ever did to deserve you, Luke Rutherford," he breathed against Luke's lips, tears rolling down his cheeks.

Luke smiled tremulously, his own eyes blurring as he kissed and licked the salty drops on Ash's skin.

"Nor I, you, Ash. Nor I, you."

He folded his arms around Ash and lay back down on the bed. They talked long into the night—about the future and all they wanted to achieve. About their wedding. About having kids, someday.

"I would want a surrogate," Luke murmured. He caressed Ash's face. "If we have children, I would love for them to look like you."

Ash smiled and pressed a kiss over Luke's heart.

Dawn was filtering through the terrace doors by the time Ash fell asleep in Luke's hold. Luke looked down at him before he closed his own eyes, his heart full of love.

He knew that they could and would face anything that life threw at them from then on. That they would overcome the trials of being in a same-sex relationship. That they would relish the challenges of growing their businesses and their family. That their friends, old and new, would support and encourage them through all their future endeavors.

That they would be together, forever.

THE END

What happens when two best friends who never thought they would fall for one another do exactly that?

Get The Proposition (Nights #6)
Turn the page to read an extract now!

THE PROPOSITION (NIGHTS SERIES BOOK 6) SPECIAL PREVIEW

PROLOGUE

I CAN FEEL HIS LIPS. HIS KISS. HIS TOUCH. THE WEIGHT OF his body on me. The lustful look in his eyes. His heat as he enters me. His strength as he takes me. His heavy breaths as he thrusts into my body.

Even in my filthiest fantasies, Wade was never like this. So rough. So demanding. So hungry. He drags me along by brute force, his giant body pinning me down to the bed while he impales me. My field of vision narrows. My reasoning is wrecked. I get muddled.

I want more.

THE WAY RHYS TAKES ME TO THE HILT, DEEP IN HIS ASS. HIS moans and his shivers as he rides me. His gasps and the way he trembles when I turn him on his front and do him doggy style. I feel like I'm going out of my mind. I have never been filled with such desire before. The desire to take. To brand.

To tame. To see him submit to me. But also to cherish. To protect. To revere.

This is more than I thought I ever wanted. So much more. And I need it all so badly I can taste him on my tongue. Yearn for him so badly that I wish this moment would never end. One thing I'm certain of.

I will never let him go.

He is my world. And I am his gravity.

CHAPTER ONE

A MUSCLE JUMPED IN RHYS DAMON'S JAW AS HE STRODE across the open plan workspace of the Tokyo branch of Damon & Tucker. He ignored the curious looks of the men and women seated at the neat, uncluttered cubicles lining the ebony floor and stormed inside a large, glass-lined office. He slammed the door shut and glared at the figure on the other side of the sleek desk dominating the stark masculine room while he flicked a switch. The outside world disappeared as the privacy glass changed from clear to frosted.

"Why did you take Misaki off the Osaka project?" Rhys snapped.

Wade Tucker placed his pen down on the file he was working on and leaned back in his leather chair. His expression grew shuttered as he locked gaze with Rhys, his slate blue eyes unreadable.

"She's not fit for it right now."

Rhys inhaled shallowly and counted to five.

Breathe. Just breathe. Don't let him get to you.

"Would you care to explain?" Rhys said between gritted teeth. "We agreed months ago that it was time to give her the lead on one of the new contracts and we did so. We're now six weeks from the deadline. The timing of this couldn't be any worse."

Wade drummed his fingers on the white laminate table, a slight frown darkening his chiseled face. Rhys found his eyes drawn to Wade's large hand and immaculately clipped nails. He wondered if Wade had touched anyone with that very hand the night before. Had dipped his fingers inside a woman's hot mouth and her wet pussy. Had gripped her ass and her hips while he thrust his hard dick repeatedly into her body.

Rhys reigned in on the torrid images flashing across his inner vision and cursed internally.

Now is not the time to indulge in your usual fuck fantasies about this dipshit.

Rhys thinned his lips, leaned against the door, and folded his arms across his chest. "I'm still waiting, Wade."

Wade let out a rueful sigh and ran a hand through his hair. "She's made several mistakes in the past two weeks that would have jeopardized the entire project had one of the other designers on her team not picked up on them."

Surprise jolted through Rhys at Wade's words. It was followed by a surge of irritation. "Why the hell didn't you tell me about this sooner? That doesn't sound like the kind of thing she'd—"

"Because I only managed to pin her down and talk

to her last night," Wade said, his own voice laced with annoyance.

Rhys stilled, his mouth suddenly dry. "Wait…please tell me you didn't sleep with her!"

Shock flared across Wade's face. He scowled and jumped to his feet, his hands flat on the desk.

"What?! *No!* What the hell do you take me for?" he barked.

"An asshole who likes to dip his stick in any wet hole he can find," Rhys said bluntly.

Wade blinked owlishly, his expression so disconcerted Rhys would have laughed had the candid statement he had just made not burned through his very core.

He'd watched Wade bed woman after woman in the sixteen years they had known each other, and it still hurt just as badly as the day he realized he wanted the man who ended up becoming his closest friend and business partner.

Fate is a sick, twisted bitch.

"You're such a fucking contradiction," Wade muttered.

Rhys stiffened under Wade's heated stare. "What do you mean?"

Wade's eyes darkened with a mixture of frustration and amusement.

"You've got that whole suave, sophisticated, butter-wouldn't-melt-in-your-mouth look down to a T," he said, his laser-like blue gaze roaming Rhys from his carefully-styled, dark blonde hair to the polished caps of his Italian loafers, "yet you've got the filthiest mouth of anyone I've ever met."

Rhys ignored the fire licking across his skin where Wade had literally kissed his body with those dangerously mesmerizing eyes of his. He unfolded his arms, pushed away from the door, and tucked his hands in the pockets of his tailor-made trousers as he strolled casually across the office. He stopped opposite Wade and faced him across the desk.

"Of course." Rhys arched an eyebrow arrogantly. "After all, that's why they call *me* The Charmer and *you* The Brute."

Wade's lips twitched at the nicknames that had plagued them since their college days. "I still maintain they should have named us The Joker and The King."

Rhys's shoulders relaxed, the tension that had been with him since that morning slowly abating. "With me in the role of king, obviously," he said tartly.

Wade chuckled, his mouth curving in a lopsided grin that brought out his dimples. Rhys swallowed a groan when he felt his dick stir in response.

Sexy fucker.

Wade's expression gradually sobered. "Misaki's pregnant. And she's thinking about having a termination," he said quietly.

Rhys inhaled sharply, surprise tightening his muscles once more.

Wade sighed. "And no, before you ask, it isn't mine."

Rhys's heart thudded in his chest as he considered Wade. "Who's the father?" he mumbled.

Wade rolled his eyes. "You get one guess."

Rhys's mind raced frantically as he thought of their staff and anyone Misaki had shown interest in of late. From Wade's words, it had to be somebody they both knew.

"Not Reo?" Rhys said. "I know she had a thing for him a while back but he just got engaged, didn't—"

"For one of the smartest guys I know, you sure are dumb sometimes," Wade interrupted, deadpan. "It's Itsuki."

Rhys ignored the insult and frowned. "We haven't got an Its—" He froze as a face swam before his eyes. "*Oh my fucking God*, you mean *that* Itsuki?!"

Wade nodded, his eyes sparkling with mirth at Rhys's stunned expression.

"The *sandwich* guy?!" Rhys spluttered. "That baby-faced kid who looks like he hasn't hit puberty yet? The one who delivers our lunch every day?!"

"Shush, keep your voice down!" Wade said with a frown, eyes darting to the frosted glass separating them from the outer office.

"We both know it's soundproof," Rhys said absentmindedly. He crossed his arms and leaned his hip against Wade's desk, still startled by Wade's revelation. "Is she serious? About the termination?" he said after a while, chewing his lower lip thoughtfully.

They both knew Misaki was deeply committed to her career at Damon & Tucker. She had been with their Tokyo branch ever since its inception four years ago.

Wade's gaze dropped fleetingly to Rhys's mouth. He sat down slowly.

"I've told her to take some time out and think about

it." He picked up his pen and rolled it between his fingers. "Her head is all over the place right now and, until she makes her decision and comes to terms with it, she won't be able to concentrate fully on work."

"Good move," Rhys murmured. He was still annoyed Wade had kept what had happened from him, but he was also pleased Wade had chosen to address things personally with Misaki first, before hauling her over the coals about her mistakes in front of the entire office. It was one of the reasons they had built such a successful business together and had fiercely loyal employees who rarely jumped ship.

"So, who are you thinking of giving the lead on the project to?" Rhys said curiously.

The pen stilled in Wade's hand. The strangest look flashed in his eyes as he gazed at Rhys.

"I thought you and I could take this one on together." A faint smile curved his sculptured lips. "Like the good old days."

Rhys's stomach plummeted as he stared back at Wade. The last thing he wanted to do with Wade was get back to their "good old days". In fact, he couldn't think of anything worse.

Rhys knew there was no way he could be that close to Wade again without doing something stupid. *Like kiss him. Or jump his bones.*

"It'll please our client. And with the both of us working on it, it won't impact too much on our schedule," Wade continued in a wary tone, as if he were testing the waters.

"What about Gabe?" Rhys said, conscious he was

grinding his teeth. He took a breath and deliberately relaxed his jaw.

"He's got his plate full with the Hawaii project." Wade grimaced. "Besides, I can practically see heart-shaped bubbles above his head whenever I look at him these days. If he wasn't a guy, I'd swear he was pregnant, too. He's positively glowing."

Gabe Anderson, one of their senior and most sought after design consultants, had recently gotten engaged to his boyfriend. Their relationship hadn't been without its trials though, and it was a testament to the two men's commitment to one another that they had come this far in such a short time.

"Well, if anyone could impregnate a guy, I'd say it was Cam Sorvino," Rhys murmured as he thought of the gray-eyed king Gabe had tamed. He smiled faintly when another man's face swam before his eyes, one he knew could also lay claim to that improbable scenario. "Or Joe Cavendish. And you, of course."

Wade startled.

Rhys suppressed a bitter smile at his business partner's expression.

"Don't worry," he drawled in the nonchalant tone he had mastered over the years of his friendship with Wade, "I know you have zero interest in sticking your dick in a man's ass." He pushed away from the desk and started for the door.

"Who's Joe Cavendish?" Wade said.

Surprise flashed through Rhys at Wade's tone. He paused and looked over his shoulder. "A friend."

Lines wrinkled Wade's brow. "You should introduce me, one day."

Rhys blinked. *If I didn't know any better, I'd say that was a hint of jealousy in his voice.* He scoffed at himself internally then. *Yeah, like that would ever happen.*

"I don't think so," Rhys said smoothly.

Wade's frown deepened.

And there it is.

Read The Proposition today

AFTERWORD

To all my friends who helped make this possible. You know who you are.

To you, my readers. Thank you for reading Ash and Luke's happy ever after. I hope you loved this fifth book in the Nights series. I would be grateful if you could leave a review on Goodreads or on the store where you purchased this book. Reviews help readers like you find my books and I truly appreciate your honest opinions about my stories.

Make sure to sign up to my store newsletter for special deals on my books and new release alerts. Or you can sign up to my author newsletter instead to get upcoming release notifications, sneak peeks, and giveaways.

ABOUT THE AUTHOR

Ava Marie Salinger is the romance pen name of an Amazon bestselling author with a passion for writing addictive tales. Known for her action-packed and thrilling urban fantasy novels, she has expanded her repertoire with the introduction of the M/M urban fantasy romance series Fallen Messengers. Additionally, she has penned the scorching hot contemporary M/M romance series Nights and Twilight Falls as A.M. Salinger. When not immersed in her writing, Ava can be found curating inspiring music playlists, indulging in her love for nature, marveling at the latest gadgets, and savoring Chinese cuisine.

You can find all of Ava's books on her author store at shop.adstarrling.com